If you are only able to read large print, you may qualify for Wolfner Library services which include free access by mail to:

- Over 350,000 titles in audio and other formats
- Use of audio playback devices
- DVDs with descriptive narration
- Over 70 audio magazines

Wolfner Talking Book and Braille Library

Email: Wolfner@sos.mo.gov
Toll free: 800-392-2614 (in Missouri)
Phone: 573-751-8720

Malice in Maggody

Malice
in
Maggody

An Ozarks Murder Mystery

Joan Hess

THORNDIKE PRESS • THORNDIKE, MAINE

Library of Congress Cataloging-in-Publication Data:

Hess, Joan.
  Malice in Maggody.
  1. Large type books. I. Title.
[PS3558.E79785M3 1987b]   813'.54   87-21045
ISBN 0-89621-834-1 (lg. print: alk. paper)

Large Print edition available in North America by arrangement
with St. Martin's Press

Cover design by James B. Murray.

For Sara Koenig, who underestimates her boundless wit and perspicacity

I would like to acknowledge the gracious assistance of the following law-enforcement officials, none of whom in any way appear in my book: Luther Hungate and his delightful wife Marsha, Ken Titsworth, J. B. Folsom, D. S. Hefner, Bud Dennis, Barry Gudgeon, Robert Gibson, and W. D. Colvard. Also, Louie Goforth, for his insights into human nature, and David McWethy, for his knowledge of the intricacies of the EPA and small-town rituals.

ONE

"It's shit — pure and simple shit, no matter what they call it in those goddamn reports," Jim Bob Buchanon said, slamming his fist down on the counter of the Kwik-Stoppe Shoppe, hard enough to rustle the cellophane wrappers of the beef jerkies. "Just 'cause some fish-brained bureaucrat at the EPA office in Dallas calls it 'suspended solids' doesn't mean it ain't shit!"

" 'Course it's shit," Larry Joe Lambertino said soothingly, "and they know it, too. But the EPA is supposed to know what they're doing, and they swear it won't affect the water quality in Boone Creek. According to them, the water from the new sewage treatment plant will be cleaner than what we've got now."

"Bunch of fish-brained bureaucrats," Jim Bob snarled. The box of beef jerkies again rustled in their plastic wrappers as his fist hit the Formica. "No, I take that back. I know a lot of fish smarter than those old boys in Dallas. The other day I caught sight of this old granddaddy catfish that must've weighed fifty pounds. He was in that pool down back of Raz's dog pen, just twitching his whiskers and watching me watch him."

"Did you try a wad of chicken liver?"

"Yeah, but that old fish didn't even blink. I swear I could hear him thinking what a goddamn fool I was to even try. But I'll be damned if I don't get him one of these days." Jim Bob paused to contemplate his chances with the venerable fish, then went to the refrigeration unit and pulled out a can of beer from the dark recesses. "Want one?"

Larry Joe shook his head. "Naw, I gotta get back to the high school. There's some PT of A crap tonight, and I need to mop the halls so the juvenile delinquents' parents can track mud all over 'em. Then I got to rush home and change clothes so that I can stand around the shop room telling them what fine potential Little Johnny has as a welder. I don't tell them he'll most likely work in a chop shop over in Platte County."

Jim Bob ran his fingers through the short stubbles of hair on the top of his head, hissing "shit" under his breath as if an unseen puncture was allowing a steady escape of air. A flash of light outside caught his attention. His eyes narrowed as he gazed through the plate-glass door at the gas pumps, and his lips pursed thoughtfully. "Look, Larry Joe, there's some damned state car out there. Wonder who it is?"

Obediently Larry Joe looked, as he always did when instructed to do so by anyone with more strength of character. It happened too often to keep track of. "Appears to be someone too stupid to figure out how to put gas in his car. You'd better send Kevin out to help him before he puts two or three gallons of unleaded down his trousers."

"Kevin!" Jim Bob roared. "Get your ass out to the pump and help that customer!" Despite his volume, he continued to gaze with a pensive frown at the scene outside.

Kevin Buchanon stumbled out of the store room, his face flushed and his prominent adam's apple bouncing in his throat like a red rubber ball. At the last second, he managed to avoid the artful pyramid of paper towels at the end of the narrow aisle. "Gee, Jim Bob, he's at the self-service," he protested in a pubescent squeak. "He's supposed to do it hisself. If he were at the full-service, then I'd be sup-

11

posed to put the gas in —"

"Get out there before I rip your ears off the side of your head," Jim Bob said without anger. "God knows it wouldn't be hard — they're almost bigger than Dahlia's jugs."

Larry Joe waited until Kevin stumbled out the door, tripped on a black air hose, recovered, and approached the white sedan with the telltale circle on the door. "That boy is a walking disaster," he said. "Him and Dahlia still playing doctor in the storeroom half their waking hours? I hope he don't put a bun in her warmer."

"The boy's a day late and a dollar short, and he doesn't have the sense to zip his fly in a tornado. Dahlia's been trying to tutor him in the manly art of screwing, but I don't know if she's actually convinced him to stick it in her yet."

Dahlia O'Neill, the girl under discussion, sauntered out of the storeroom, a half-eaten candy bar in one hand and a rolled magazine in the other. The dark blue tent draped over the three hundred pounds of flesh was dusty and wrinkled, but her face was as serene as that of any madonna who had recently submitted to immaculate conception. "How you doing, Mr. Lambertino?" she said in greeting as she went behind the counter.

"Go check the soda pop supply," Jim Bob said.

"Checked it this morning." She popped the last bit of chocolate into her mouth and daintily sucked her fingers. Her bovine eyes remained on Larry Joe.

"Check it again. There's lots of kids in on Friday afternoon," Jim Bob said, turning back to the door. "Now that's a car from the inter-agency motor pool. Sure ain't the governor, sure ain't the highway commissioner or no tax man from the state revenue office. Just who do you reckon it might be?"

Larry Joe shrugged, his bony shoulders hunched as though he were taking the shape of a long-range missile. He did not, however, look nearly as lethal. "I don't know why you're so all-fired interested in that car and that fellow. He looks real ordinary to me, Jim Bob. He's probably some fool paper pusher from Little Rock."

Before Jim Bob could offer his thoughts, Hobert ("call me 'Ho' ") Middleton pulled up, his flashy black Cadillac shuddering as he slammed on the brakes inches short of the leaded, regular, full-service. It took a few seconds for him to extricate his plump body from behind the steering wheel, managing during the process to leave his lush gray hair unscathed. He tugged at the crotch of his plaid trousers as he entered the Kwik-Stoppe Shoppe.

"Hey, Ho," Jim Bob said. "You look more worn out than Dahlia's public access ramp. Want a beer?"

Hobert flapped a newspaper under Jim Bob's nose. "Did you have a chance to look at the Starley City paper this morning?" Hobert demanded in a melodious voice that rippled with indignation. "On the front page, just under the story about the Miss Starley City beauty pageant."

"A story about the beauty pageant?" Larry Joe said, leaning over Jim Bob's shoulder to look at the newspaper. "Joyce and I almost decided to go, but one of the boys upchucked on the middle of the living room carpet and she had to stay home so she could clean it up. It liked to never come out of the green shag. Is there a photo from the swimsuit competition?"

Jim Bob made a noise in his throat. "Listen to this, Larry Joe. It says that the EPA office in Dallas has finally agreed to Starley City's application, and they're going to let them sign the construction contract with that firm up in Kansas City. They're sending a contract approval fellow up today to finalize the deal, and they're hoping to break ground real quick."

"Shit."

"You got it — or you're going to, right soon." Jim Bob paused to read in silence, his lips quivering over the longer words. "It talks about the public meetings and the petitions and protests we sent, but it says that the EPA office has evaluated the so-called community input and environmental impact reports and decided to approve the application anyways. In a year or so those chickenshits in Starley City will be dumping their suspended solids in Boone Creek. I'll have over a hundred acres of frontage on a sewage ditch, and that old catfish will belly up before I can catch him."

Hobert took back the newspaper and tucked it under his arm. His face, somewhat mottled at best, turned a deeper red. "That's right on the button, Mr. Mayor. I got nearly that many acres myself, and I don't like shit any better than you. Now, exactly what do you aim to do about it?"

"I put in another call to Senator Fiff, but he's still on his fact-finding mission to Las Vegas. Be back Tuesday, according to some snippety secretary with the charm of a pig getting castrated. If he can't stop this, I don't think we have a grasshopper's chance in a hen house. Next time this year

15

we'll be flycasting for turds."

Kevin came back into the store, followed by a slender man in a three-piece suit. The man handed Kevin a ten-dollar bill, nodded to the three men watching him, and disappeared down one of the aisles. With a youthful thirst for knowledge, Kevin headed for the storeroom.

Jim Bob inclined his head in the man's direction. "He's got a car from the state pool, Ho. You know what I think?"

"You think he's from the Dallas EPA office? One of those engineer fellows who's been coming up here all year to take water samples?" Hobert Middleton was nobody's fool. He reminded people all the time, if they thought otherwise.

"It says in the paper that Starley City is expecting someone today to approve the contract at some damn fool ceremony at the city hall. I think that's him. State car, polyester suit, slick expression. Bet you a case of Bud that's the man what's going to deliver the shit to Boone Creek. We got to think of a way to stop him from okaying the construction contract until Fiff gets hisself back from Las Vegas and throws a monkey wrench in this mess."

"You honestly think Fiff can do some good?" Hobert asked.

"I don't know, but it's our best goddamn

16

shot. Once everything is signed and tied up in pretty pink ribbon, we can whine as loud as we want, but nobody'll listen." Jim Bob poked a finger into Larry Joe's concave chest, which was conveniently at eye level. "Keep that government man here till I get back. I'm going to go fetch Roy Stiver so we can have a quorum for a special meeting of the town council."

"A special meeting?" Hobert raised two bushy silver eyebrows. "I don't have time to stand around, Jim Bob. I got a fellow bringing in a load of new models and I need to be there to make sure the merchandise ain't dirty or damaged. I got a reputation for selling the cleanest cars in the county, you know —"

"Back in a minute." Jim Bob hurried out the door and cut across the driveway toward a row of buildings.

The man thought to carry the desecration of Boone Creek in his briefcase found a path out of the aisles. Blinking in the fluorescent glare, he cleared his throat and said, "The young man who pumped my gas said I could heat a burrito in the microwave. Would either of you know exactly how to operate it?"

Larry Joe and Hobert nodded.

Raz Buchanon stomped into the police department, his watery, red-rimmed eyes snapping and his whiskery chin several inches ahead of his nose. An aroma of sourness swept in on his heels. "Perkins stole my dawg, Arly! He plumb took it right out of my pen, and I want to know what in blazes you plan to do about it!"

I put down the block of wood I was whittling into a semblance of a duck. "Now, Raz, you need to calm down. How do you know Perkins took your dog? Maybe the dog jumped the fence and went looking for a bitch in heat."

"The dawg is a bitch — and that son of a bitch took her." Raz glanced around for a can to spit in. He settled for a dusty corner and sent out a glistening amber stream.

I will admit I winced. Having been the chief of police for more than eight months, I should have grown accustomed to such things. Some things may take years. "Do you have any proof to back your accusation, Raz? I can't just arrest Mr. Perkins and send him to the penitentiary on your say-so."

"You can, too. Perkins is a low-down lying thief; everybody in the county knows it but you, Arly Hanks. He done it so that he can run the dawg during deer season and pretend it's one of his from the last litter. I know for a fact he ain't had a decent dawg in two years." One cheek puffed out ominously, then receded.

"Ain't had a deer, neither," he added with a cackle. He looped a misshapen thumb through the strap of his overalls and waited for me to join in the general merriment.

"I have to have proof."

"The hell you do! Jest ask Jim Bob if Perkins ain't a dawg thief. I'm guessing you'll take the word of the mayor."

Would you take the word of the mayor of Maggody, Arkansas, population seven hundred fifty-five?

"You can sign a complaint if you want to, Raz, and I'll send Paulie out to Perkins's place to investigate. But I can't file charges unless the dog is discovered on his property." I took out a form and pushed it across my desk.

Raz wiped his mouth on the back of his hand as he stared at the complaint form. "Iz that paper for dawg thieves?"

"That's right," I replied with a sober expression. "I have a different one for each species of stolen animal. This one is for dogs. If the animal were a cat, I'd use the green form." It was, of course, nonsense, but Raz couldn't read a word of it. I had to do something to amuse myself during the eight-hour shift.

"You jest send Paulie Buchanon out there to get my dawg," Raz said, backing toward the door. "I don't need some damn fool paper to

19

say Perkins stole Betty."

"Officer Buchanon will report the facts of the case at his first opportunity," I said. "In the interim, stay away from the pen so that you won't destroy any evidence. We may need to make plaster casts of the footprints and dog residual in order to convict Mr. Perkins of this heinous kidnapping charge."

"I got to feed the other dawgs. How in thunderation am I supposed to do that if'n I stay away from the pen?"

I gave the dilemma serious thought. "The only solution, Raz, is throw the dog food from your back porch. Otherwise, Perkins will get away with the crime and you won't be able to regain custody of Betty."

Raz showed me two toothless gums. "Thankee, Arly."

"My pleasure, Raz." I picked up the block of wood, which had not transformed itself into anything remotely resembling a duck. Perhaps an elephant, or dog residual. The creative juices were clearly not bubbling, so I put my knife away and replaced the wood in a drawer. I then opened my purse, reapplied lipstick, breathed on my badge and polished it with my cuff, and went to see my mother.

Ruby Bee's Bar and Grill is situated at the north end of Maggody, exactly one-half mile from the south end of Maggody, which gives you an idea of the entire scope of said town. Unlike more picturesque communities snuggled in the verdant valleys of the Ozark Mountains, Maggody despondently straggles along both sides of the state highway. After the half mile, it peters out with a few dilapidated billboards and a sign that welcomes Rotarians, Lions, Kiwanians, and Masons. Maggody possesses none of those, but it does strive for a friendly note.

The population has decreased steadily since the turn of the century. I know from personal experience that the dream of every Maggody teenager is to move away as quickly as possible and, with luck, never come home again. Some do; others never quite find the nerve to venture into the land of dragons and freeways. Yes, I did, and I ended up back where I started, at least for a time while I recuperated from an ugly divorce and a bad case of the ego-shakes. After all, my advertising hot-shot ex-husband did leave me for a model who specialized in foot commercials – dear Veronica something-or-other of the sculpted toes. I wished them happiness, herpes, and bunions in what used to be my Manhattan co-op, dining on my china and sipping champagne out of my crystal goblets. I walked out empty-handed but with my pride intact. No one uses much crystal in Maggody.

I'm the chief of police only because I was the one and only qualified person to apply after the last chief snuck out of town with Dahlia O'Neill's older sister. Paulie Buchanon applied, but the town council felt obliged to take me. Paulie hasn't been to the police academy yet, while I'd done so and also had several years of experience with a private security firm. Nothing to do with police work, naturally, but I didn't share that with the town council. Hell, I needed some entertainment while I sorted things out. It was a good thing I didn't need much money.

If all the Buchanons are confusing to you, good luck. Half the residents of Stump County are Buchanons. Inbreeding and incest have produced the beetlish brow, beady amber eyes, and thick lips. Nothing in the way of intelligence has been produced. Buchanons are known for a certain amount of animal cunning, but nothing that would outwit an above-average raccoon. The other half of the Maggody PD and my loyal deputy, Paulie Buchanon, is smarter than most of his relatives; he's terribly sincere and determined to escape Maggody via the state police academy. Jim Bob's no dummy, either, if holding the office of mayor for thirteen years is any indication. He pulled enough horse trades to put up the Kwik-Stoppe Shoppe (known to locals as the Kwik-Screw) and to build a big brick house on a hilltop overlooking Boone Creek. He may have made an error when he married Barbara Anne Buchanon, his second cousin from over in Emmet. Everybody calls her Mrs. Jim Bob, a local and inexplicable tradition that's not worth dwelling on.

Ruby Bee's, as I mentioned earlier, is on the north end of town just before the skeletal remains of Purtle's Esso station. Once you pass that, there's nothing worth looking at until you reach the Missouri line, unless you like staring at cows. Ruby Bee's is a low concrete-block building painted a curious shade of pink and decorated with metal signs extolling the virtues of Pepsi-Cola, Royal Crown Cola, and something called Happy Daze Breads and Buns. There is a six-unit motel behind the bar, although no tourist has found the courage to actually stay there more than an hour. It's called the Flamingo Inn; there's still one solitary plastic flamingo posing under the sign that says *V can y*. Ruby Bee resides in Number One so she can keep an eye on the activities that take place after midnight. The locals refer to it as the Maggody Stork Club. Work on it.

I parked my patrol car in front and called the

county sheriff's dispatcher to let her know I'd be out of town for lunch. She wasn't especially interested — could be because I get a message from the dispatcher maybe once a month, and that for a vehicle accident. Due to the vigilance and alertness of the Maggody PD and the ennui of the residents, there is no crime. As I got out of the car, I decided after I ate I'd run a speed trap by the school zone sign until it was time to follow the school buses to the county line. Or maybe at the signal light. Such decisions.

Did I mention that the infamous Ruby Bee is, among other less enchanting things, my mother?

"Ariel, honey, what's wrong?" she called as I stepped into the cool dimness of the bar. It's a good-size place, with booths along one wall and a few tables scattered around a handkerchief dance floor. On Saturday nights it's jammed with good old boys at the bar and girls dancing with their eyes closed, mouthing the words of the songs while they picture themselves on the Grand Ole Opry stage.

"Nothing's wrong," I said irritably. "I came in to eat lunch, not to collapse of malaria on the barroom floor." I pulled myself together and managed a smile. "Sorry, but this place is starting to close in on me. I really thought I knew what I was doing when I moved back. The only thing Maggody and Manhattan have in common is a couple of letters of the alphabet, but I'd forgotten how quiet things are around here — along the lines of a mouse pissing on a cotton ball. Do I look all that bad?"

"You just look so pale, honey. Why don't you wear a little more makeup?" This from the woman who wears alternating stripes of pink eyeshadow, black eyeliner and mascara, and scarlet lipstick. I probably did look pale through her eyes. Her blond hair (worth every penny of it) and girlishly white complexion gave her painted features a rather ghostly look, as though she hovered behind the bar. Her body was substantial but reasonably trim for a woman who refused to get out of bed on the day of her fiftieth birthday — five years ago.

"It's mere malnutrition," I promised, "and soon to be alleviated, if you feed me." I told her about Raz and Perkins while she dished up a plate of pork chops, rice, gravy, and fried okra.

"Raz is just being ornery," Ruby Bee informed me as she brought a glass of milk to the bar. "Perkins whupped him in checkers three nights running and won seventy-five cents."

"Did he purloin poor Betty for revenge?"

"Probably, but Paulie ain't going to find the

bitch until deer season's over." My mother has her finger on the pulse of Maggody. Her sweet round face invites confidences, which she promptly repeats to anyone who'll listen, including me. There's not much else to do in Maggody. While we were discussing ways to rescue the victim, Ruby Bee's dearest friend, Estelle Oppers, came in and joined us.

Estelle is as tall as I am (five-feet-ten in my socks) and as skinny (135, soaking wet and no socks). She is not pale, however, and no one has ever suggested she add more color to her violet eyelids or to her fire-engine red hair, arranged that day in sort of a Grecian column effect. She is the proprietor and sole operator of Estelle's Hair Fantasies, located in the living room of her house. Every female in Maggody has at one time or another found herself in Estelle's chair − except me. I prefer to maintain my dark hair in a sensible bun. Trimming is done with cuticle scissors and provides most of my excitement on weekends.

Twenty years ago Estelle played the piano and warbled in a motel lounge in Little Rock, our state's major metropolis. With enough sherry pumped into her, she still reminisces about her promising career that was cut short by some obscure tragedy. According to her, when she got warmed up she could put every customer in tears with her rendition of "Moon River." I don't doubt it for an instant.

Estelle bellied up to the bar beside me and gave me a puzzled frown. "You look different, Arly. Did you finally do something to your hair?"

"I combed it, but that's about all. Why all this concern about me out of the blue, ladies? I can swear on Grandpappy Hank's Bible that not one tiny thing has happened to me — or anyone else I know — in a coon's age." I tried to return to my pork chop.

The two exchanged meaningful looks, then Ruby Bee took over. "Estelle and I was just thinking that, and I don't mean to insult you, you're looking a little peaked these days, honey. You work all day, then sit around that dreary apartment all night instead of getting out to have some fun. You could go to the dance over in Kingsley next Saturday and meet some young people like yourself."

Estelle bobbled her head. "Sure you could, Arly. I'd be real pleased to do your hair for free. Maybe even frost it with a burnt gold rinse, then —"

"Thank you, but no thank you," I interrupted. "I'm fond of my hair as is, and I have no desire to attend the bimonthly festivities at the Kingsley high-school gymnasium. I would be fifteen years older than ninety-nine percent of those in attendance, and sixty years younger than the remaining one percent."

Ruby Bee began to pout. "You used to go every time."

"I used to be in high school, and that was all there was to do. I am now thirty-four years old, divorced, and the chief of police. The kids are probably still sneaking out back to drink corn liquor out of mason jars and throw up on each other. It wouldn't look good for me to attend. You don't want me to lose my job, do you?"

"That would be just awful," trilled a voice from behind us. Jaylee Withers ambled into the room, her generous hips moving to an inaudible rumba and her well-endowed chest bouncing along with the beat. Her blond hair had recently been exposed to Estelle's artistic whimsy, for it was piled higher than a run-of-the-mill beehive; it literally soared a good twelve inches. I was surprised she wasn't trailed by a homeless swarm.

"We were talking about the dance in Kingsley," Ruby Bee announced, giving me a dark look. "I was telling Ariel here that she ought to get out and have herself a good time, but she thinks she's too old and respectable to listen to me."

Ruby Bee drives me crazy.

Jaylee nodded with all the wisdom of a twenty-two-year-old married woman currently employed as a barmaid. "She's right, Arly. If you stay home, you're gonna get all sour and dried out, like Raz's oldest girl. Then no man will have you and you'll spend the rest of your life in Maggody, dreaming about fancy cars and fur coats."

"Raz's oldest girl is sixty-seven years old if she's a day," I pointed out. "Furthermore, I've already had fancy cars and fur coats. I never could find a place to park, and my nose itched every time I even opened the closet door."

Jaylee was too busy winking at Ruby Bee and Estelle to be swayed by my logic. "You know, Arly, I'd be charmed to do something with your hair, free of charge. I need the practice for when I attend cosmetology school, hopefully as soon as next month, if I pass the GED this time. Estelle's been teaching me and I could do a right nice French roll for you. You could come by my mobile home tomorrow and I could give you a permanent, then I could —"

"Sorry, I'm on a case," I said. The pork chop was too cold to bother with, anyway. "An investigation into a kidnapping that could have profound influence on the deer season — although it's strictly under wraps for the time being. I'd better get back to it."

I left Ruby Bee's, knowing full well that I hadn't fooled any of them. I could almost hear them dissecting poor Arly's situation — so tragic, you know. The way she drags around and she ain't ever going to catch another man. You'd think she'd have enough sense to forget that man in Noow Yark and settle down with someone who could give her a houseful of kids and an automatic dishwasher, a night at the picture show once a month and a lifetime subscription to *Better Homes and Gardens*.

I climbed into the police car, slammed the door, and snatched up the mike on the police band radio. "Chief of Police Hanks has returned to active duty. Ten-four, seven-eleven, and Bingo!"

Estelle and Jaylee drive me crazy, too.

Paulie Buchanon was sitting in his cruiser in the shade next to Roy Stiver's Antiques and Collectibles: *Buy, Trade or Sell*. I pulled up next to him and rolled down my window. "What the hell are you doing, Officer Buchanon? Unless there's been a change in the roster, you don't come on duty until six o'clock tonight. Since I make up the roster, which hasn't varied in eight months, I have some doubts."

Paulie Buchanon did not deserve my testiness, which he knew as well as I. He gave me a wounded look and said, "I was just keeping an eye on the signal light, chief. Jim Bob cussed me out for not writing more tickets last month and acted like he was going to fire me."

"His Honor can't do that without consulting me first," I said, turning my glare on the Kwik-Screw across the street. "He'd have to call a special meeting of the town council, and they'd have to vote on it, anyway. Did you catch anybody running the light?"

Paulie held up a book. "No, actually I was studying the state police manual."

"Did you hear from them?" I asked sympathetically, forgetting my feud with His Honor the Moron. "A result from the test?"

"No, but it'll be any day. They're processing my exams and interviews now, and said they'd let me know by the end of the month." Paulie's eyes glazed over as he considered his future as a state policeman, and even the skin on the top of his head seemed rosy under the sparse black hair. "Do you think I ought to get me a pair of those mirrored sunglasses, Chief?"

"Wait to be accepted at the academy," I advised him, determined not to giggle. Paulie's terribly sincere, especially when the topic centers on the academy. "Why don't you go study at the PD while I nab perpetrators at the signal light? I was thinking about it earlier, and it'll help me burn off a little frustration."

Paulie grinned at me, having seen me drive away from Ruby Bee's at a velocity above that permitted within the confines of Maggody. "Sure, Chief. Holler if you get bored and I'll take over for you."

He left, and I backed around to park in the shade. Another thrilling afternoon in Maggody, where nothing has happened since Hiram Buchanon's barn burned down eleven years ago and a cheerleader got caught running out of it, smoldering pink panties in hand.

T W O

Paulie came in the next afternoon to report that Perkins refused to cooperate in the investigation. The dog had not been spotted among the children and chickens playing in the dirt in front of the ramshackle cabin. "I suppose I could go back with a warrant," Paulie concluded morosely, "but Perkins'll probably dump a load of buckshot in my behind. I don't think he's got the dog, anyway."

"Probably not," I said. "We can decide about a warrant next Tuesday when the municipal judge shows up for court. I'm sure as hell not driving all the way into Starley City to get a search warrant for a dog, especially Raz's bitch."

I leaned back in the chair and studied the ceiling while Paulie bustled around the back room, fixing coffee and playing with the radar gun. He'd make a fine space explorer; I could hear him making little noises under his breath as he zapped aliens and cockroaches. I suspected I'd sort of miss him when he left for the state police academy, but I was praying hard he'd get accepted.

The police band radio sputtered to life. I fiddled the knobs and settled back for another exciting communique from the sheriff's office, expecting to hear that some damn kids had smashed themselves up on the hairpin curves north of town.

I was wrong. When the radio quieted down, I stood up and brushed the dust off my khaki fanny, then hollered for Paulie. "I need to run over to Ruby Bee's," I informed him with a grim smile. "Carl walked off the prison farm sometime yesterday. We're supposed to keep an eye out for him, but I think I'd better warn Jaylee right away."

Carl Withers was once Maggody's main claim to fame, when he won all-district mention in football. The recruiters did not swarm to town to offer Cadillacs and scholarships, however, and he ended up working for Hobert Middleton in the body shop. He managed to impregnate Jaylee during her sophomore year of high school (he was twenty-six at the time) and did the honorable thing, although she lost the baby a couple of months after the wedding. Two years ago he'd tied one on, stolen a brand-new Eldorado off Hobert's lot, sideswiped a Buchanon child on a motorscooter, and totaled the car just outside of town. The child ended up with two broken legs and a concussion. The judge was unamused and Carl got four years at Cummins State Prison Farm down by Pine Bluff. Among his other talents, Carl was bigger than a semi and meaner than a water moccasin. A real live sumbitch, as we say in Maggody.

When I found Jaylee, she was in a back booth, studying a cosmetology magazine for inspiration. She choked on her tongue when I told her Carl was loose. After a great deal of coughing and tearing, she got hold of herself and managed a shaky laugh. "He wouldn't dare show his face around here, Arly. He'll go to his brother's house in Texarkana and then head south. He used to talk all the time about getting a job on one of those oil rig things in the Gulf of Mexico."

"I hope so. I looked up the file on him before I came over here, Jaylee. He beat you up pretty bad the night he got arrested, didn't he? Seven stitches in your lip and a fractured collarbone?"

Ruby Bee was listening from behind the bar. "That's the unvarnished truth," she inserted, having no reservations about butting in. "It wasn't the first time neither. I saw you plenty of times with a split lip, Jaylee, or wearing sunglasses to hide a shiner. That Carl's a skunk if I ever met one."

Jaylee's lower lip edged out, as if she were going to protest, but she thought better of it. "He can be rough," she admitted. "That's why I was hoping to be long gone before they let him out of jail. I figured he'd never be able to find me in Little Rock."

I was nudged aside by my deputy. "Hey, Jaylee," he said as he sat down across from her and reached for her hand. "You don't have to worry about Carl showing up in town. The state police and the sheriff's department are both watching for him, and if he makes it here, he'll have to deal with me first."

In that Paulie had snatched the words right out of my mouth, I retreated to the bar and ordered a glass of milk. Paulie sat with Jaylee for a long time, murmuring too soft for me to catch more than a tadpole's tail of what he was saying. Jaylee finally relaxed and stopped trying to wiggle her hand free. Their heads moved closer, and I could see she was fanning him with her eyelashes.

"Sweet, ain't it?" Ruby Bee cooed over my shoulder. She's a sucker for soap operas and romance novels.

"Just like molasses. Maggody's cutest couple, making plans to escape before the demented husband shows up with a twelve-gauge to blow them both to smithereens."

"You think Carl'll head this way?"

"Beats me. I don't know him — the Withers family moved here after I graduated from high school and left for college. He must be a real prince, though." I finished my milk and glanced over my shoulder. Jaylee was showing Paulie one of the more fanciful hairstyles in her magazine while she tugged at the curls dangling over her forehead.

"It's Saturday," Ruby Bee said in an innocent tone. "You got any plans for tonight?"

"I'm going to get drunk and shout obscenities out my bedroom window," I said as I started to leave. "Is Robin Buchanon still making hooch up on Cotton's Ridge? I might run up and get me a couple of jars."

Ruby Bee snorted delicately. "I don't keep up with Robin Buchanon, missy. She's a slut and she doesn't even try to guess who fathers those filthy brats of hers. She must have ten or eleven by now, in all different shapes and colors."

"Enough for a touch football team. I'm going back to the police department to see if there's any word on Carl or Betty. Send Paulie along when his hand gets so sweaty he can't hang on anymore."

To my regret, I met Jim Bob and Hobert in the doorway. Jim Bob glared up at me and said, "Don't you have any work to do, Chief? The town council doesn't pay you to hang around bars gossiping with the womenfolk."

Hobert's pendulous chin quivered in agreement. "I saw three out-of-town cars run the signal light this morning, Chief. If you don't write some more tickets, you may find yourself with a down-right skimpy paycheck at the end of the month."

"I was just on my way to check dealer tags with the state license department," I said politely.

I pushed past them and went to my car, a little surprised by the virulence of the attack. There's no love lost between the town council and me, but we usually keep civil tongues when I appear to beg for a new box of pencils or a junior G-man fingerprint kit. They laugh, I laugh, and we adjourn till the next meeting. I'm always the last item on the agenda. It lets them wind up the meeting on a light note.

Larry Joe and Roy were pulling up in Larry Joe's pickup as I drove away. It seemed that all the local dignitaries were gathering at Ruby Bee's Bar and Grill, which was odd. The other two members of the town council were not present, but neither had made a meeting in several months. Harry Harbin was visiting his daughter in Miami Beach and wasn't expected back until his arthritis eased. Old Jesse Buchanon was around somewhere, but he was so senile he couldn't stop dribbling long enough to find the meeting room.

I hung around the office the rest of the afternoon, working on the duck and filing my nails. Nobody called in with any information about Carl Withers, so I assumed he'd headed for Texarkana and points south. At six o'clock Paulie arrived to man the night shift. He was still pink around the gills from his session with Jaylee, whom he adored almost as much as his badge and radar gun.

"Did Jaylee feel better when you left, Officer Buchanon?" I asked sweetly.

He had the grace to blush. It was quite appealing on his boyish face; he's the sort who'll look eighteen when he's forty-five, even though he'll be balder than a coot's ass. I'll have all my hair and look fifty-five.

"No word on Carl," I said as I started for the door. "You can call the dispatcher if you want to, but I doubt she'll have anything for you. Carl's likely to be in New Orleans by tomorrow."

"I'll handle him if he shows up," Paulie said

in a low voice. If he was doing an impersonation of John Wayne, I missed it.

I walked across the highway to my apartment, which is above Roy Stiver's antique shop. Maggody has a limited number of rental units, and I wasn't about to move back home with Ruby Bee. There were several mobile homes available at the Pot O'Gold Mobile Home Park, but I lacked the moral fiber to live in a structure at which God aims tornados about once a month every spring. That left a tent or Roy's apartment, which was dirt cheap, catty-corner from the police station, and not too bad if you squinted and used forty-watt light bulbs.

Roy Stivers is an interesting old guy and a good landlord. Like the rest of us, he returned to Maggody when he got tired of life in the fast lane, but he stayed gone thirty years while his mother ran the antique store. It's one enormous room, colder than a witch's tit, and crammed full of glassware and old books. The tourists stop a lot, thinking they can pull a swift one on grizzled old countryboy Roy. He chaws around with them, playing the rube, and reluctantly lets them buy an old table for twice its value. I'm the only one who knows he writes poetry in the little office in the back of the store. He had a volume of poetry published about twenty years ago. I read it, but most of it was above my head or below my knees — I never could decide. Roy and I occasionally sit around the stove and drink bourbon. I noticed he wasn't around as I climbed the stairs behind the store.

I was working on a bowl of chicken noodle soup when the telephone rang. It was Paulie, and he was rattled. At last I determined that a real live state trooper was actually in our office, being officious and demanding to see me. I grabbed a jacket and strolled across the highway, not about to be intimidated by someone in mirror sunglasses.

He wasn't wearing the sunglasses, perhaps because we operate at an economy-minded wattage. I could see why Paulie was rattled, however; the guy was putting on a pretty darn serious show.

"Chief of Police Hanks? I'm Sergeant Plover, State Police."

"I saw your cruiser outside," I said as I slipped behind my desk. "You parked too far from the curb, but I'll let it go this time." A little joke — we don't have any curbs in Maggody.

He was a big man, as tall as I am but decidedly broader across the chest. I'm more vertical than horizontal myself. He looked to be about forty or so, his face chipped like a dish from the dump and his nose doing a zig where it should have zagged. Blond hair (longer than regulation, I'd have bet), brown eyes, and a smattering of freckles. He might have been all right when he smiled, but he sure wasn't at the moment.

"I appreciate your professional courtesy," he said, although he didn't sound real sincere. "We have a small problem, and I was sent to request your cooperation, Chief Hanks."

I propped my feet on the desk and grinned. In one corner of the room Paulie was slumped against the wall, gulping harder than a salmon going upstream, but I ignored him and kept my eyes on the trooper. "Sure, anything at all. I'm always willing to cooperate with the state police — you all are the ones who never ask me to dance. Does this have something to do with the escaped convict?"

"No, we'll get him before he reaches your jurisdiction. If he tries to hitch north, one of our boys will be polite enough to give him a ride back down to Pine Bluff. You don't need to worry about that."

What he meant was that I didn't need to bother my pretty little head with such scary things — it was plainer than day in his eyes and tolerant smile. "Ooh, thank you," I squeaked, producing a girlish shiver. "I'll sleep better knowing that you'll catch that big nasty man before he gets to Maggody."

"Will you? That's good to know."

Paulie was now hopping from foot to foot, probably convinced I had destroyed his chances for the big time. I decided to ease up just a tad, since I didn't have a good excuse for my behavior anyway.

"Then what did you have in mind in terms of cooperation, Sergeant?" I smothered a yawn and blinked up at him.

"We had a call from the regional EPA office in Dallas. They sent a contract specialist up this way yesterday to meet with the city council in Starley City, but the man failed to arrive. The council finally called Dallas this morning to find out what happened. Dallas had no idea anything had happened, but they called us. We agreed to run a check, and learned that" – he took a pad from his pocket and consulted it – "one Robert Drake signed for a car from the interagency motor pool yesterday at eight-sixteen in the morning. He told them he would return it today and return to Dallas on an afternoon flight. That was the last anyone saw him."

"Good," I muttered. When Sergeant Plover gave me a sharp look, I added, "No one in Maggody is excited about Starley City's proposed sewage treatment plant on Boone Creek, which runs west of town. I've read all the environmental impact reports, and I know they say the water will be cleaner than it is now, but I don't like the idea of sewage flowing through my old swimming hole."

Sergeant Plover thought that one over for a minute. "So the citizens of Maggody are angry about the proposed plant. Would anyone be likely to prevent Mr. Drake from reaching Starley City?"

"No one put up a roadblock yesterday, if that's what you're getting at," I said. I picked up a pencil and rolled it between my hands. "The EPA has already made the decision and granted the construction application. Starley City is going to build the plant whether we like it or not, so I can't see anyone making a grandstand play with some little bureaucrat whose job is to sign some paper. They'd just send someone else, wouldn't they?"

"You and I know that," Sergeant Plover murmured, trying to include me in his mental meanderings. "Well, I'd appreciate it if you'd ask around town, see if anyone saw a state car or this Drake man."

"I'll ask, but it won't do any good. He's probably holed up at some truck stop with a CB hooker or taking his sweet time driving up from Little Rock. Maybe his car broke down." I shrugged to emphasize my heartfelt disinterest in missing EPA men and state troopers.

"That has already occurred to us. He would have contacted someone or touched base if he experienced car trouble. We've checked all the motels on the highway between here and Little Rock, but he may have eluded us." Sergeant Plover touched base with the visor of his hat. "In any case, my visit is just a formality, Chief Hanks. We don't expect you to produce the missing man. You're hardly equipped to deal with that sort of thing, are you – you and your deputy, I mean?"

I wished I had Robert Drake stuffed in my bottom drawer; I really did. "Of course not," I said to the back of the state trooper. He was through the door before I could add an expletive or two.

Paulie slunk out of his corner. "Do you think you should talk that way to the state police? What if they. . . ?"

"What if they what, Officer Buchanon? They can't take away my badge or make me turn in the radar gun." I broke the pencil and let the pieces clatter to the floor. "I would like to find the errant EPA man and hand him over on a silver platter to Sergeant Plover, however. What are the chances the missing man stopped in

Maggody and found himself so in love with the town that he couldn't bear to leave?"

"About one in ten million."

"Agreed." I sat and brooded for a few minutes, then took my feet off the desk and stood up. "Maybe Drake stopped to pick up a hitchhiker in a zebra suit. Carl murdered him, changed clothes, stole the car, and is now driving to Starley City to sign their paper. He'll then report to work in Dallas Monday morning."

"I don't think so," Paulie said, frowning. "Most people won't stop for hitchhikers these days. Too dangerous. While I'm on patrol tonight, I'll ask around and find out if anyone saw the car go through town."

"Let me know if you find out anything." I returned to a bowl of cold chicken soup. I spent a delirious hour watching the news and learned that Carl was at large and possibly armed. Nobody had mentioned that tidbit to me. I spent another equally delirious hour at the front window watching the pickup trucks and beat-up Chevies cruise up and down the highway, the kids hollering and honking at each other.

Even that paled. I put on my jacket, crammed my hands in my pockets, and walked down the road to Ruby Bee's, trying not to think of my former life, when I spent my Saturdays at intimate dinner parties, offering politically correct opinions over martinis. One beer, I decided, then bed.

Ruby Bee's was humming, as usual. The bar was blocked by a solid row of denim jackets topped with cowboy hats. Very little neck in between. The jukebox moaned and wailed at top volume so everyone would know he was having a good time. After a cursory glance to see if I saw anybody I wanted to sit with, I elbowed a path to the bar.

If I had thought my mother would be delighted to see me out enjoying myself on a Saturday night, I was wrong. When she finally got around to me, she gave me the expression she had used when discussing Robin Buchanon's propensity for reproduction.

"What are you doing here?" she demanded.

"Having fun. Drinking beer and being sociable. You're the one who told me to get out and do something."

She gave me a funny look and a fast beer. "Here's your order. You don't have to stay here on my account, Arly. If you'd rather be home reading or something, don't feel obliged to linger."

It's heartwarming to know you're always welcome at your mother's. "Let me drink my beer before you throw me out, okay?"

"Nobody's going to throw you out. I just don't want you to put your nose out of joint because of some dumb thing I said yesterday." Ruby Bee began to wipe the counter with a vengeance. "I don't know why you started taking my advice, anyway. You never did before."

My eyes were getting rounder by the second. The lip of the beer bottle fit right in the circle my mouth made as I stared across the bar at a woman who was trying her damnedest to pick a fight with me. "What are you gabbling about?" I asked.

"Well, I told you not to run off to Noow Yark with a man that writes those television jingles, didn't I? I knew you wouldn't like that kind of life and those people."

"And you were right, weren't you? I scampered back with my tail between my legs, just like you said I would. I let you say 'I told you so' five hundred times in the last eight months and never whimpered."

Ruby Bee wiped the counter hard enough to leave a rut in it. "I did tell you so. You should have listened to me." She was going to continue in that vein, but the cowboys around the bar were ready for another round. She snapped the rag under my nose and left. I picked up the bottle and squeezed away from the bar to find a table where I could analyze the conversation for hidden undertones.

I bumped into Estelle, who was carrying a tray with a forest of bottles. "Why are you working?" I yelled over the music. "Where's Jaylee?"

Estelle shrank back and stared at me as if I had a third eye in the middle of my forehead. When I repeated myself, she managed to come to her senses. "I'm just helping out for a few minutes; Jaylee was feeling poorly and went to lie down till she felt better. What are you doing here?"

I held up the beer bottle. "Same thing everyone else is doing, I guess. Is something wrong around here that I don't know about? Did Carl show up?"

Estelle jerked her head back and forth. "No, not a trace of him. I wouldn't lie about that, Arly. He's a real nasty fellow and he's likely to go after Jaylee and hurt her. I swear on a stack of Bibles I'll call you if Jaylee hears one word from Carl or sees one hair of him."

That sounded sincere. I nodded and went to sit with a married couple I knew from high-school days. Alex and I drank beer, but Charlene stayed with RC colas in a glass, rubbing her swollen belly with a satisfied expression every now and then. I learned number three would be ripe in a couple of months and that they were hoping this one would be a boy so they could name it after Alex's father.

It wasn't especially exciting stuff, and I kept an eye on Estelle as she waited on tables and chatted up the customers. She, in turn, kept an eye on me, as if she thought I was going to pull out my gun and blast the jukebox. Alex and Charlene wandered home to rescue the babysitter, leaving me alone in the booth to wonder if I would end up like Raz's oldest girl.

After an hour, Jaylee suddenly appeared in a short apron and took the tray from Estelle. Jaylee looked unharmed; in fact, she looked as satisfied as Charlene had when touching her belly. I curled a finger at her for another beer, and when she approached, I asked her point-blank if she'd heard from Carl.

"Gawd, no, I'd be home locked in a closet if I heard from him," she said with a shudder that set her breasts in motion for several seconds afterward. "I learnt my lesson the last night he beat me up, and he knows I wouldn't give him the time of day if he got down on his knees and begged. I just hope they catch him right quick and lock him up for about twenty years."

That theory wasn't holding water, much less beer. Sergeant Plover might have been right about Carl's chances of making it all the way to

Maggody. As I thought unkind things about Plover, I noticed Jaylee's hair was rumpled and a button had been torn off her blouse. The lace-edged napkin pinned above her left breast was wrinkled down so that her name was invisible.

"Estelle said you were sick," I said cagily.

Jaylee chewed on her thickly coated lower lip. "I went to lie down for a few minutes, but I feel fine now."

"A touch of the stomach flu?"

"Something like that, yeah. I got to get back to work, Arly. These old boys get pissed if they have to wait for beer. You going home now?"

I was not exactly a hit in Ruby Bee's Bar and Grill that night. I said I was going home to listen to Mozart, waved halfheartedly at the wretched woman who claimed to love me as only a mother can, and left.

Outside it was cold and crisp, a perfect autumn night with the crackly acid smell of leaves turning brittle and pine burning in far-away fireplaces. Back in the hills deer were moving around cautiously and possum waking up for a bit of nocturnal mischief in barns and garbage cans. Owls waiting for mice and squir-rel to go too far from the nest. Bears lumbering around to find a last berry patch before settling down for the winter. Chiefs of police sulking in the shadows to spot an escaped prisoner and show up state troopers.

There were at least two hundred more stars in the sky in Maggody than there were in Manhattan, I decided as I cut across the Kwik-Screw lot and climbed the steps to my apartment. As I reached the top step, I heard voices from somewhere below. Sounds can carry a long ways in the cold night air, but I at last figured out they were coming from Roy's back room.

In my dual capacity as conscientious renter and police officer, I tiptoed back down the steps, wishing I had my gun with me in case I found some damn fool prowler in Roy's store. I cocked my finger and whispered "Bang, bang" as I moved around the corner and stood on my toes to peek through the back window.

I caught sight of the proprietor in person as he moved across a patch of light, a bottle of bourbon in one hand and four glasses in the other. If it was a party, I pointedly hadn't been invited, so I scurried away and retraced my tracks to the top of the steps. I might have been feeling just a tad sorry for myself as I crawled into bed and yanked the covers over my head. A social outcast in Maggody tends to feel that way.

THREE

Robert Drake leaned back against the pillows and opened a magazine. The cheesecake did little to ease his growing boredom; he had tried the television earlier, but the Sunday-morning preachers were foaming away about hell and damnation, two of his least favorite subjects. With luck, a football game might come in on one of the fuzzy channels in a couple of hours. Maybe even the goddamn Dallas Cowboys and those lusty, busty cheerleaders. God, he hated the Dallas Cowboys.

A key rattled in the door, and a sugary voice yelled, "You decent, Robbie?"

He threw the magazine on the floor and deftly unzipped his fly. Then, pulling off his glasses and rumpling his hair, he said, "Sure am, honeybee, and about to starve to death. Come on in."

Jaylee opened the door, a tray balanced on one hand. She carefully locked the door behind her and dropped the key down the front of her blouse. Robert could see it wasn't going anywhere he wouldn't like to go himself. "I brought you some breakfast and a newspaper like you asked," she said. "Did you sleep —" She caught sight of his fly and wiggled her eyebrows. "Thought you said you was decent."

With a puzzled frown, Robert followed her gaze. He waited for a minute so she could enjoy the view, then fumbled with the zipper. "My apologies, Jaylee. I guess I was dozing off, since there's nothing else to do in this jail cell. It's obvious I'll never make a very good kidnap victim."

Jaylee put her free hand on her hip. "Now wait just a blessed minute, Mr. Robbie Drake. You have not been kidnapped. Jim Bob says you are being delayed for a few days, and he's the mayor so he ought to know. Nobody's going to cut letters out of a magazine for a ransom note or make falsetto telephone calls to your office. On Tuesday you can be on your way to Starley City just like you planned."

"I know that, honeybee, but Tuesday is forty-eight hours away. What am I supposed to do in the meantime — get religion watching some paunchy preacher on television?" Despite his aggrieved tone, he was smiling. His fingers plucked at the wrinkles of sheet next to him.

Jaylee put the tray down and pulled off the aluminum cover. "Well, for one thing you can eat your breakfast. I brought you eggs, grits, ham, biscuits, a couple of buttermilk pancakes, and coffee."

"That doesn't sound bad, but I can think of something I'd prefer," he said silkily. His hand had crept back to the zipper, and he scratched a fingernail along the metal teeth to make a noise, in case she hadn't noticed. Sometimes honeybees needed a little guidance. "It seems to me you might remember what I like if you lie down beside me and concentrate real hard."

Jaylee giggled. "It may come back to me later, Robbie, but right now I've got to run along home and change clothes for church."

Robert Drake realized that his presumed morning delight was going to center on biscuits rather than breasts. Scowling, he reached down for his magazine and jerked it open to the centerfold. "Have a nice time in church," he said, silky having transformed to sulky. "Don't even stop one minute to think about me locked in this crummy motel room without anyone to talk to." It was worth a try.

"Oh, Robbie," Jaylee said with an indecisive frown, "I'd like to stay and visit, but I have to

55

teach my Sunday-school class in an hour. We're doing a special study on Jonah and the whale, and those kids'll be real disappointed if I don't show up. I promised them a flannel board story. I've got real cute little figures that I cut out of a workbook, with sandpaper on the back so they won't fall while I'm telling the story."

Robert kept the magazine in front of his face. "Have a good time. God knows I'll be right here whenever you see fit to bring me a glass of water or something."

Jaylee sighed. He sounded so lonely lying there, pretending to be brave even though he was frightened and in need of warmth and comfort. In fact, she thought with another sigh, he sounded like one of the little boys waiting for her at the Voice of the Almighty Lord Assembly Hall. She noted the time on her watch and came to a decision. "I can stay a few minutes, Robbie, but then I got to get home and change. Brother Verber'll be peeved at me if I'm late; the boys stir up mischief if they're not supervised. Fifteen minutes — not a second more. Okay?"

Seventeen minutes later she did up the last button on her blouse and waggled a finger in farewell. "I'll come by right after church so I can bring you Sunday dinner. You be a good boy till I get back, you hear?"

"I'll be here," Robert mumbled from under a pillow. The sheets were tangled around his legs and the blankets pushed off the end of the bed. The bed felt damp and smelled ripely sour, but that was the way he preferred it. "You give a real fine whale story to your Sunday-school class, honeybee."

She left after a few deep, soulful looks that went unheeded. Several minutes later he realized he was hungry, hungrier than a damned whale. As he shoved back the sheet, a key fell from between the folds and bounced off his foot.

Robert picked it up and rubbed it between his fingers as he pondered his options. He could, if he wanted to, throw his clothes in his suitcase, grab a biscuit, and make his escape from the dismal room. The shithead yokels had probably left the keys in the car, if he could figure out where they'd parked it. No doubt everybody would be holed up in church, bellowing hymns and basking in a self-righteous glow that would keep them holy for most of the week.

Within an hour he could be at the state police headquarters to file a kidnapping charge. Hell, he'd make them call in the FBI. Then the clowns who'd had the nerve to pull a rifle on him two days earlier and march him into the back room would find out it wasn't so damned smart to tangle with Robert Drake. He'd pick them out of a lineup, wait till they were locked up in some rathole of a jail cell, and be on his way to Starley City. Sign the contract approvals in the morning and fly back to Dallas after a couple of martinis in the airport bar and a bit of grab-ass with the stewardesses. Be back in time to stop at the office and humbly accept praise for surviving the ordeal. Maybe even make the ten o'clock news with that smarmy woman reporter with the big tits and wet, full lips.

None of which, except for the final item, struck him as the thing to do. The office was thick with assholes who might laugh at him. God knows his wife Dawn Alice would, she and her bitchy friends. He could almost see them having Sunday brunch at the country club. Dawn Alice would be having a wonderful time in the role of distraught wife, shredding Kleenexes between bloody marys and boo-hooing on the tennis pro's shoulder while he fondled her buns and whispered obscenities in her ear. Would she even pretend to be relieved when he strolled in like a Greek soldier home from the war?

"Bitch!" he snarled. He put the key under the bed and arranged a corner of the sheet to cover it. Then, whistling softly as he remembered his prowess playing Jonah to Jaylee's whale of a fine, ripe body, he pulled a chair up to the round table and began to butter a biscuit.

I usually eat breakfast on Sundays at Ruby Bee's, but I wasn't about to stick my nose in there until I received apologies from several different parties, all of whom had been snootier than a nursery-school teacher the previous night. I boiled water (one of my talents) for instant coffee and dumped a mound of cornflakes in a bowl.

After the nutritious if not scintillating breakfast, I wasted a couple of hours cleaning the apartment. The yellowed linoleum was still yellow when I gave up, but it was clean. I then gathered up my dirty clothes, crammed them in a pillowcase, and walked to the Suds of Fun laundromat beside the Kwik-Screw. No one had called to beg forgiveness or even to see if I was alive.

I sorted the clothes, plopped various piles in the row of washing machines, and dug through my pockets for enough quarters to coax the machines into doing the dirty work for me. A beanpole with acne shook his head when I asked for change, so I went into the Kwik-Screw.

Dahlia O'Neill was perched on a stool behind the counter, her eyes glued on the interior of a tabloid that promised the inside scoop on aliens knocking up Colorado housewives. A pile of candy wrappers sat on the counter next to a Nehi bottle.

"Let me have three dollars worth of quarters," I said, putting the appropriate number of bills down.

"Hey, Arly," she said. "How you doing?"

"I'm doing fine, but my clothes are getting dirtier by the second. Quarters?"

"Jim Bob says I ain't supposed to give change unless you buy something, 'cause this ain't some goddamn branch of the Chase Manhattan Bank." She turned to the next page and reached for a candy bar from the rack. It was nearly empty.

"I realize that this is in no way a bank," I said patiently. "My first clue was that the Kwik-Screw is open on Sunday and the Chase Manhattan is closed. I'll buy a newspaper, okay?"

That got me a newspaper, a nickel, and two quarters. A candy bar got me three more, and a bag of potato chips another two. I decided I could run the dark colors with the wash-and-wear, and to hell with the towels. If they turned to mildew, I'd come back and rub Dahlia's face in them to get them clean. Not that it'd work.

I took my change and trophies and started to leave, then stopped and turned back. "Hey, Dahlia, did you happen to see a white Ford in town Friday around noon? It had a painted circle on the door, a state seal."

Dahlia looked up, the flesh under her chin squashing out so she resembled a walrus. No tusks, but a noticeable mustache. "Yeah, I seen it. Cute little fellow tried to fill it up, but he couldn't figure out how to work the pump. Kevin had to go do it for him, even though it was self-service and costs two cents less. Jim Bob was real pissed about it."

"Did you see the car leave? Which way did it go?"

"Can't say I noticed," she said, flipping to another thrilling story of sex and intrigue among the Hollywood stars. "You might ask Kevin, if you see him."

"What time was it when the car stopped here?"

Dahlia belched softly, then pounded her chest with her fist. "Nehis get me every time, sorry. I don't recollect what time that was. I was unpacking some boxes in the storeroom and I can't get my watch around my wrist no more. You might ask Kevin if you see him."

I was beginning to get the message: Ask Kevin. I tried once more for luck. "But Jim

Bob was here when the fellow in the state car pulled up, you said. Could he have noticed which direction the car pulled out?"

"I dunno, Arly. He sputtered around for a while, then banged out the door like he had a Roman candle up his ass. I decided to finish unpacking in the storeroom, and I didn't see Jim Bob come back or anything. I suppose you could —"

"— ask Kevin," I interrupted, nodding. "Where is Kevin, by the way? I'm surprised Jim Bob gives him a day off."

Her sad, crescent eyes grew round as my stupidity reached her brain. "He's at church, Arly. His mama makes him go every Sunday just like clockwork. She says she'll wallop the living tar out of him if he screws up his perfect attendance record and loses out on a genuine gold lapel pin."

I went back to the laundromat and rearranged the loads. Then, feeling as if I'd made a smidgen of progress with the case of the kidnapped bureaucrat, I grabbed the newspaper, settled back in the plastic chair, and turned my attention to the happenings outside Maggody. They seemed about as real as Dahlia's little green men with their busy green pricks.

I ate a substantial lunch of chocolate and chips, dried my clothes, and went back to my apartment. I had just won my third game of solitaire Scrabble (I cheat) when Paulie called. I knew from the tremor in his voice that we had a visitor in the office. My uniform was clean and ready, but I left it in the closet. My gun and holster made me look on the bulgy side, so I didn't bother with them. If you have to know, I did slap on a little lipstick before hurrying across the highway. It didn't mean a blessed thing.

"They certainly work you hard in the big time," I said to Sergeant Plover as I sat down behind my desk and aligned the telephone book with the edge of the desk. "Nights and weekends. Do they let you off on Mother's Day?"

"I'm off in the middle of the week, which is fine with me. Too many crazy people with guns in the woods on weekends. I prefer a little peace and quiet." He sounded easy, but his smile seemed forced. "Have you discovered any information that might assist my investigation, Chief Hanks?"

Paulie began to shake his head, but I held up my hand to prevent any incoherent sputters from his direction. "Make some coffee, please, Officer Buchanon; my mouth feels like the inside of a clothes dryer. Yes, I have, Sergeant Plover. The car in question was seen by a convenience store clerk on Friday, sometime close to noon. I haven't completed the interrogation, and there is still another witness to be located, but I think I can file a report by tomorrow."

Sergeant Plover rewarded my brilliance with a terse nod. "Have the report on my desk by five o'clock this afternoon. Include the addresses of the witnesses so that I can question them myself."

"I told you I would question them."

"I'm sure you will, Chief Hanks, but this case has become top priority. The car has been found."

I guess he thought I would *ooh* and *aah* and tell him how smart he was. I took my duck out of the drawer, instead, and studied it for signs of progress. "That was lucky. Where'd it turn up?"

"On a logging road in the national forest, halfway between here and Starley City. What's that supposed to be?"

I twisted the block of wood around so he could see the most promising side. "A duck. A male, marshland mallard, to be precise, but I just started on it. Any evidence of violence at the scene?"

"It doesn't look like any duck I've ever seen. Where's its head?"

"I told you that I just started. What are you — some kind of closet ornithologist?" I dropped duckie in the drawer and slammed it closed. "What about the car, Sergeant Plover? Fingerprints, footprints, tufts of hair, what? And last words written in blood on the windshield?"

Sergeant Smartass Plover slapped his forehead. "We forgot to look! I'll send someone right back to see if we missed a ten-foot suicide note or a treasure map or something like that. Thanks, Chief Hanks — you may have broken the case. I want you to know you have the undying gratitude of the Arkansas State —"

"Stuff it," I said, as I got up and started for the door.

He put his bulk between me and the screen. "Wait a minute, Chief. Why don't we forget all this and start over? I'd like to tell you what we did find, and discuss the case with you. Drake was last seen in Maggody; he never made it to his appointment in Starley City. I'm beginning to think something may have happened within your jurisdiction, which means you and I will have to cooperate on the investigation."

"The investigation?" I echoed, still more pissed than a polecat.

"Our investigation." He gestured for me to sit back down and went so far as to take his hat off, gentleman that he was. I studied his thick hair and what Estelle would call its burnished gold highlights, with a few strands of gray above his ears. I'd thought all state troopers had boot-camp hairdos that looked like old currycombs glued onto shiny pink billiard balls.

In the back room Paulie whooshed like a balloon. I dragged my eyes back to business and pasted on an expectant smile. "Well?"

"The car was found early this morning by a hunter who was out scouting for a stand. There were no signs that Mr. Drake had not left the car voluntarily. Whatever luggage and brief-cases he might have had with him were gone. The ashtray was half filled with cigarette butts, his brand, and a bottle of bourbon was under the driver's seat, down a couple of inches." He pulled out a county survey map and showed me the thin line that petered out in the national forest. "Here, about two hundred feet from Boone Creek."

"But why would he park in the middle of nowhere and leave the car?" I asked. "That doesn't make any sense. The road stops at the water, and the only people who park there are kids looking for a little privacy to smoke dope, drink beer, and eventually have a roll in the hay — or brambles."

Sergeant Plover studied the wall a good six

inches above my head. His ears reddened and his voice sounded tighter than a fiddle string as he said, "We did find evidence of past — ah, carnal activities along the road and at a clearing near the bank. Rusty beer cans, too, and cigarette papers."

It was good to know the youth of Maggody took precautions when they threw caution to the wind. "Could Drake have gone there with someone he picked up?" I asked.

"That's what I've been wondering, but you know more about the local — ah, hitchhikers than I do. If he was alone when he stopped for gas at the convenience store, he must have found his — ah, friend somewhere in Maggody or just past the city limits." The ears were getting redder by the minute and looking like they might burst. "I was hoping you could suggest some possible — ah, residents with a reputation for — ah, drives in the woods, and —"

I did not want to watch his ears burst, since it might add splatter to the already fly-specked decor. "There are a few women who would have hitched a lift and hiked their skirts in exchange for a monetary reward. Officer Buchanon and I will ask around town. I may be too busy with that to have a report on your desk at five o'clock, but God knows I'll try my darndest. Is that all?"

"One more thing, Chief Hanks. Do you have a first name? I need it for my report."

Like a bull needs a tutu. "My first name is Chief. What about yours, Sergeant Plover?"

"Sergeant." He stomped out, forgetting to ease the screen door closed or even say goodbye. A few minutes later, he drove away at what I estimated to be about sixty-five miles per hour, and in a twenty-five-mile-per-hour zone at that. Tut, tut.

The dust was still swirling when I left the PD to find Kevin Buchanon. A rumble from my stomach reminded me that I hadn't had a decent meal all day. Figuring that Kevin would be busy with fried chicken and mashed potatoes for another half hour, I walked down the road to Ruby Bee's.

The parking lot was empty, and Estelle was the only body at the bar. She gave me a cool nod as I sat down beside her. Ruby Bee came out of the kitchen, a dish towel in her hands. "Whatcha want, Arly?"

The pariah of Maggody had been hoping for an apology. "A grilled cheese sandwich and a glass of milk, if it isn't too much trouble." The two exchanged a few of the secretive looks that were beginning to get on my nerves. "I'll fix it myself if you're not in the mood," I added coldly.

Ruby Bee managed to fake a smile. "No, you stay there and visit with Estelle. I'll make you a sandwich. You don't have to come in the kitchen at all, Arly."

The chef bustled out of sight, clucking under her breath like I'd demanded steak au poivre. Estelle managed to fake the very same smile, which went about one flea-leg deep. "So how are things, Arly? You interested in trying that highlighter or mebbe a frost? I think it'd come out real sweet on you, help soften your face and give you more of the feminine mystique."

"I'm still screwing up my courage, but I appreciate the offer, Estelle. I know I can count on you as a true friend, someone who'd never hide anything from me or pretend to —"

"Arly, what are you doing here?" squeaked Jaylee, from the doorway. She wobbled in on spike heels, her prim navy dress doing little to disguise her less-formal curves. She wore a white hat with a blue ribbon and carried white gloves in one hand.

"You must have come straight from church," I said, trying to sound impressed. "Aren't you going to have trouble waiting tables in those heels? You're likely to trip and dump a bowl of gravy in someone's lap."

She looked wildly at Estelle and then at the

kitchen door. "I didn't come in to work," she said, twisting the gloves. "I just dropped by to – to – study! That's all, Arly."

"You can't study in the comfort and solitude of your mobile home in the Pot O'Gold Mobile Home Park?"

"No, I – I needed some help with the formulas for frosting hair, and I wanted to ask Estelle." Jaylee looked down at the remains of her gloves and stuck them behind her back. "How long you planning to stay, Arly? You going to be here all afternoon?"

It was the damnedest thing. Estelle was swallowing like she'd stuck a piece of gum halfways down her throat, and Jaylee was blinking and teetering like she had to pee in the next five seconds. I stared at them, more bewildered than I'd ever been in my whole life.

Ruby Bee sailed into the silence. "Why, Jaylee, what a pleasant surprise to see you here this afternoon." She was as convincing as the lead in the first-grade pageant. Jaylee ran through the "study" explanation, giving me quick little glances the whole time to see if I was buying it, then looked at Ruby Bee for further inspiration.

"I believe I found something of yours in the kitchen," Ruby Bee said to her, looking straight past me. "Why don't you come see if it belongs to you, Jaylee?"

Estelle gave the blond a shove. "That's right, Jaylee, Ruby Bee and I were almost sure it was yours, but you'd better go look at it."

Jaylee blinked for a moment. "Oh, right," she chirped at last. "I'll go in the kitchen with you and see if it's mine or someone else's. See you later, Arly." She teetered away on Ruby Bee's heels.

"She drop her brains in the kitchen?" I asked Estelle. "It's no surprise she hadn't noticed till now."

Estelle looked down her nose at me. "Now, Arly, you shouldn't talk about Jaylee that way. She's had a hard life, but she's a good girl and she's determined to make something of herself. I've told her many a time she has a real flair for hair design and that she'll be a real fine beautician once she gets a license. Not everyone is smart enough to go to college and live in Noow Yark." She sounded as if she placed Noow Yark somewhere south of Zaire.

"And she hasn't heard from Carl?"

"I told you I would call if she did. I swear, you're acting very peculiar these days, Arly, sniffing around like you think there's something funny going on at your own mother's place of business. If I was your mother, I'd be offended — I sure would."

"What'd I do?"

71

Estelle snorted an answer and stuck her nose in a glass of sherry, making it clear I wasn't worthy of her conversation.

It didn't look like I was going to win Miss Congeniality that day. When Ruby Bee stomped out of the kitchen and slammed down a burned cheese sandwich in front of me, I meekly ate it without offering an editorial. I never did get a glass of milk, much less an offer for a piece of cherry pie with ice cream. And when Jaylee scooted out the door with a covered tray, trying to pretend she was heading for the ladies' room for a quick snack, I ignored it.

But I noticed. The three weren't exactly subtle with their hints, which were closely akin to direct requests to move my behind out the front door and stay away. I wondered if they were planning a surprise birthday party for me but reluctantly let that one go, since my birthday was in February. I just wished I knew what was going on, that's all.

FOUR

I drove out Finger Lane to Kevin Buchanon's
house. His mother situated us in the living
room, and his father gruntingly allowed himself to be talked into dish-towel duty in the
kitchen. Kevin was still in his Sunday suit and
tie, but it just made him look all the more
pitiful in contrast. He stared at me, his mouth
slightly open. His throat was rippling like his
nostrils and adenoids were having a tennis
match.

"I'll only take a minute of your valuable
time," I said, resisting an urge to pinch his lips
closed before he caught a mouthful of flies.
"What can you tell me about a white Ford that
stopped at the store Friday morning?"

"It had circles on the door."

"Good, Kevin. That's the very car I'm interested in. Dahlia said you had to assist the man

at the pump. Did he say anything to you?"

Kevin took an ominously deep breath and let 'er rip. "He said he never could figure out how to work the gas pumps, but it didn't matter because he never used self-service much anyway. Then he said the front tire looked low and for me to check it and look under the hood. I said at the self-service he was supposed to do it hisself, and I needed to fill up Mr. Middleton's car before I did anything else, but he said he wasn't about to get oil on his clothes and for —"

"After you finished with the professional discussion, did he say anything about his trip?"

"He said he hadn't had anything to eat all day but a sweet roll on the airplane and could he get something inside the store. I said he could get a better deal at the Dairy Dee-Lishus next to the high school, 'cause they make real tasty cheeseburgers and frito pies, but he said he was in a big hurry and that he needed something right then." Kevin sucked in another deep breath. "Then he said to check all the tires while I was at it, and he went inside to get a burrito and a diet soda. I told him that the burritos were better than the ham-and-cheese sandwiches 'cause the delivery man comes every other week to exchange them. I tried a sandwich once that cracked my tooth and the delivery man told me it had happened before once in —"

"Did you see him after that?"

"The delivery man?"

I took my own deep breath and reminded myself that Kevin was a vital witness in my investigation. "The man in the white Ford, Kevin. Excluding all references to food, gasoline, and tire pressure, did you hear him say anything else?"

Kevin screwed up his forehead, looking for all the world like a chimpanzee who'd had experimental, unsuccessful brain surgery. "No, I don't believe I did, Arly. I got busy doing something else, and when Jim Bob came to tell me he was leaving for an hour or so and to stay in front in case someone needed full-service, the fellow was nowheres that I could see. I don't guess I thought any more about it until you asked me."

Or anything else, I amended under my breath. I thanked Kevin for his assistance and drove to Jim Bob Buchanon's pretentious brick mansion on the hill. Mrs. Jim Bob met me at the door and placed me on a hideous turquoise sofa in the front room, saying that they were almost finished with dinner and she'd send Jim Bob out to visit with me shortly. I sat with my hands in my lap and my ankles crossed, feeling like a candidate for homecoming queen who was about to be measured by a bunch of football players. I had just finished counting the eyelets in the doily on the end table when Jim Bob came into the room. There were eighty-eight. Eyelets, not mayors.

"Chief Hanks, what a pleasant surprise in the middle of my Sunday dinner," he said, halting on the K-Mart genuine Oriental rug, and folding his arms. "I saw a state police car parked in front of the police department yesterday and again this morning after church. Did you come to make an official report to me?"

"Actually, I came to question you." I would have bitten my tongue in half before I'd call him Mr. Mayor to his face. Or Mr. Buchanon, or anything else that was half-civilized. "The state police contacted me about a fellow from Dallas who disappeared Friday on his way to Starley City. Dahlia and Kevin both confirmed that you were at the Kwik-Stoppe Shoppe when the man stopped for gas. I need to find out which direction he went and if he might have indicated any plans not to continue on to Starley City."

Jim Bob gave me a smile that was pure smirk. "I have a lot of customers every day, Chief Hanks. I don't waste my time chatting with them or asking them about their itineraries like I was a travel agent."

"But you were there Friday around noon?" I persisted. "Did anyone else come in while the man was there?"

"I didn't notice. I thought of something I needed to tell Roy, so I left myself. Unlike yourself, I am a very busy person and I take my responsibilities to the community as a heavy burden. Although I make it a point to attend church on a regular basis, unlike other people I won't mention, most of my time is spent trying to balance the budget and make sure that our citizens receive the services they deserve — including police protection."

I opened my mouth to protest, but he cut me off with the second half of the lecture. "I suggest you let the state police worry about that fellow from the EPA, Chief Hanks. You might spend more of your leisure time making sure the schools are free from drugs and that the speeders don't run down some innocent Maggody child who's crossing the street to buy a stick of candy."

I could hear my blood beginning to simmer, but I managed not to let it gurgle out my ears. "If you feel I am not doing an adequate job protecting the citizens of Maggody, why don't you just say so and fire me? Then your second cousin twice removed can take over as chief of police, and you won't have to worry about the crime rate."

"Now, listen here, young lady, if your mother wasn't a friend and lifetime resident, I'd apply my boot to your bottom so fast you'd still be feeling the dent six months from now!"

"Oh, yeah?" I said cleverly, sticking my chin out so he could get an eyeful of my dimple.

"Jim Bob Buchanon," Mrs. Jim Bob said from the door, "I cannot believe my ears. You have no business speaking to Arly in that tone of voice, and I'd like to think good Christian gentlemen don't go around kicking ladies anywhere. Now you just apologize right now if you intend to have a piece of my pecan pie for dessert."

Jim Bob weighed the evils, looking pretty darn unhappy. Finally, when Mrs. Jim Bob was on the verge of repeating her demand, he glared at me and said, "I don't kick ladies, so I most likely wouldn't kick you, either. Why don't you skedaddle back to your office and do a little police business, Chief Hanks?"

It was not the most eloquent apology I'd ever heard, but it was all I was going to hear in the turquoise room. I flashed my teeth at the Buchanons, gave Jim Bob a big wink to show no hard feelings, and left them to peace and the pecan pie.

When I got back to the PD, I found Paulie behind my desk. He was in a spiffy uniform, right down to the gun, and looked a lot more professional than his boss, who was traipsing around in a cloud of dust.

"Anything happened?" I asked.

He shook his head and sighed. "No, and today's Sunday, so it's not likely anything will happen. The state police called to say that someone claimed to have seen Carl Withers down toward Arkadelphia, but they hadn't been able to confirm the report yet. Guess that means he's too scared to show up here."

"Or too smart." I gestured for him to vacate my chair, which he did with a rumble of embarrassment. "Was it Sergeant Plover who called from the state police?" I asked nonchalantly, leaning over to get my duck out of the drawer.

"No, some lieutenant from the Little Rock division. Did you find out anything from Kevin?"

"More than I ever wanted to know about leaky tires and burritos." I then gave him the general gist of that conversation and the subsequent one with His Honor the Moron, and waited patiently until he stopped gasping and making faces. "I've got an idea, Officer Buchanon. Let's run out to the logging trail

79

where the car was found and see if we can stumble onto any evidence that was overlooked by the state boys. It's a nice day, and there isn't anything else to do. We might even find something."

"The crime scene?" Paulie said, excited. "Do you really think we might find a clue?"

"We're more likely to find used condoms and poison ivy, but you never know." I replaced the duck in its drawer and we left. It did too have a head.

"I'll never forget my sixteenth birthday party," Jaylee confided, her head on Robert's shoulder. "I really thought it was going to be the start of a wonderful life, what with all the balloons and a big cake with pink flowers and a circle of teensy pink candles."

Robert took a drag on his cigarette and stubbed it out in the ashtray on her stomach. "Good party, huh?" he said through a yawn. "Spin the bottle and that sort of crap?"

"It was a real nice party. We had little sandwiches with the crusts trimmed off and punch made from ginger ale and sherbet. I wore a pink dress that was right out of *Seventeen* magazine. My parents agreed to stay away so we could dance without being self-conscious."

She continued to relate each and every detail

of the party, to Robert's disgust. It must have been a real bash, he thought snidely as he lit another cigarette and produced an occasional murmur of amazement or encouragement. He reminded himself that he was paying dues for the more interesting activities that had kept him amused most of the afternoon.

His eyes were almost closed when she said, "But, after my girl friends left and I was cleaning up, that's when Carl came over and practically raped me right on the carpet in front of the television!"

"Raped you, huh? Did he rip your clothes off or what?" Robert enjoyed the details of such things, although he would never do anything like that himself. He figured he was too smart to end up in jail when he could have all he wanted without any arguments.

"Well, you know," Jaylee said, suddenly reticent just when he was getting interested. "Then I found out I was pregnant, so I told Carl and he said he'd marry me. Two months after a real sweet ceremony in the Voice of the Almighty Lord Assembly Hall, I miscarried the baby. Now, ain't that the most ironic thing you've ever heard in your whole life, Robbie? There I was, Mrs. Carl Withers, and no baby after all!"

The flicker of heat in his loins turned to ice. "You're married, honeybee? I don't remember you mentioning that minor fact before. Where's Carl at the moment?"

Jaylee giggled as she drove her head into his shoulder. "Who knows? He could be right outside the window watching us this very minute, getting all hot under the collar. He's mean enough to chew up nails and big enough to swallow them." While Robert silently sweated, she went on to describe some of Carl's more vicious fights and the carnage that had resulted. "He escaped from prison two days ago," she concluded with another giggle, "and they can't find him. He could have gotten a ride up this ways and been hiding in the woods, waiting for a chance to make me give him some money so he can go down south and find a job on one of those oil rig things."

Robert lit another cigarette off the one trembling in his hand. Husbands, particularly brutish ones with bad tempers, made him nervous. It was one thing if they were out of town on some damn fool business trip, leaving the little woman alone and lonely for male companionship. But a husband of the escaped-convict category was another thing. Another thing indeed.

Jaylee crawled over him, doing a good job of smushing her breast across his stomach as she grabbed for the bottle on the floor beside the bed. "Can I make Robbie baby a little-bitty drinkie?" she lisped, flapping her eyelashes and pouting. It had driven him to distraction less than an hour ago.

"Make Robbie baby a big fat drink. Make yourself one, too." Hell, what were the chances the junkyard dog of a husband would ever stumble on to the love nest in Number Three of the Flamingo Motel? He had thirty-six more hours of being kidnapped, and he might as well enjoy it. Let honeybee work off the sin of omission. He slapped her bottom as she climbed out of bed. "You hurry right back to bed so your Robbie baby won't get lonely, you hear? You wouldn't want me to have to spank you again for being a bad little girl . . . "

Paulie and I got back to the office just before dark. I was covered with scratches, itchy, sweaty, filthy, and generally unhappy with the results of our tree-to-tree canvas of the neighborhood. We'd found exactly what I predicted, along with three dozen empty beer cans, two pairs of panties, and a copperhead with a nasty glint in its eye. Groaning, Paulie told me he was going home to shower and change clothes. I suggested iodine for the scratches.

As I dragged my poor body up the stairs behind the antique store, I noticed Jim Bob's four-wheel, Larry Joe's truck, and Hobert's Caddie all parked in a tidy row by the back door. I wearily wondered if Jim Bob had called a special meeting of the town council so he could tell them about my visit and get me fired. I wearily decided I didn't give a shit and headed for the shower and the iodine bottle.

Jaylee's head was back on Robert's shoulder once more, and her mouth was flapping like a pair of jeans on a clothesline in a gale. Robert had learned he needed only to murmur every once in a while to keep her happy. When she ran down, he stuck his finger in his drink and flipped a few drops on her stomach just to hear her squeal.

"No wonder Dawn Alice gets so all-fired mad at you," she said, giggling as she dried herself with a corner of the sheet. "But I don't know why she ain't happy being married to you, Robbie. You're more than enough man for any woman. I sure wouldn't waste my afternoons at some snooty country club; I'd be home in the kitchen cooking your dinner and waiting for you to come home from work."

"Guess what I'd do when I got home?" He put his drink on the rug and demonstrated until she pleaded for him to let her rest up for a few minutes. "When are you moving to Little

Rock, honeybee?" he asked while he reached for his drink. "I have to go there maybe once or twice a month and I might be able to squeeze in a night with you in your little apartment."

"I should hear tomorrow in the mail if I passed the GED. They say the third time's a charm, and I've been crossing my fingers and toes like a fool. If I do pass, I'm going to throw everything I own in the back of my car and leave this dump in fifteen minutes flat. I already got accepted at the Purley Institute of Hair Design and Beauty, and they said I could start whenever I got my equivalency diploma and showed up on the doorstep."

Robert realized that he might not enjoy being kidnapped if Jaylee weren't around to keep him occupied. The shitheel mayor and his three stooges had come by a couple of times, wanting to talk about the proposed sewage treatment plant and their precious creek. As if he cared. He had pointed out that he was only a lowly contract specialist and had no clout except over clauses and exceptions, but they didn't seem convinced. Sure, he could delay the contract for a week or two. It would get signed eventually, and there wasn't a damn thing they could do about it.

He grabbed a handful of Jaylee's hair and pulled it back until he could see her face. "You mean you might leave tomorrow? What am I supposed to do — play with myself?"

"Aw, Robbie, they're going to let you go Tuesday." She winced as his fingers tightened. "Stop it, please. Somebody'll bring you trays and magazines after I'm gone — maybe Estelle or Ruby Bee herself. I'll tell her to cook something real special for your last night, and even bring you a bottle of wine to go with dinner."

"Big frigging deal." He freed his hand and idly slid it down her neck to her breasts while he tried to decide what to do. A wonderful idea finally broke through the bourbon haze. "Tell you what we're going to do, honeybee. When you find out if you passed whatever the deal is, you pack the car and drive right over here to the door. You unlock the door and get back in the car, then I'll jump in, hunker down in the back seat until we're out of this rathole of a town, and ride with you to Little Rock."

"I don't know, Robbie. Jim Bob would be real perturbed if —"

He rolled on top of her and covered her mouth with his lips. "You just do what I say, honeybee," he muttered between kisses. "We'll stop in some motel to spend the night, and I'll —"

She twisted her face aside. "But Jim Bob told

me that delaying you was the only way to keep Starley City from —" She broke off with a scream loud enough to wake up the bodies in the back room of the funeral parlor.

Robert leaped off her and took refuge in a distant corner, just in case she was planning to go nuts. "What's the matter with you? Why'd you have to go and scream like that?"

Jaylee grabbed the sheet and covered herself. She marched to the door and yanked it open. "You goddamn sick pervert!" she yelled into the darkness, her buttocks atremble with indignation. "You know you're sick, don't you — watching people through the window! I hope your pecker gets snagged on a barbed-wire fence!"

"You saw someone at the window?" Robert gasped. He snatched up a blanket and wrapped it around himself, feeling as if he were in some department store window with a crowd of gawkers on the other side of the glass. "Who — who was it, honeybee?"

Jaylee slammed the door and swung around. "I didn't get more than a quick peek, but I can tell you it was some filthy pervert! The idea of him staring at us while we was in bed makes me want to puke. He was probably drooling and playing with himself, like some crazy person in an institution for the criminally insane."

"You didn't recognize him?"

Jaylee shook her head, then dropped the sheet and began to dress. Robert poured himself a drink, gulped it down, and refilled the glass, wishing his hands would stop twitching. "Could it have been Jim Bob or one of those guys checking on me?" he asked.

"I told you I only got a peek."

Robert gulped down the second drink. "What about your husband Carl? Could it have been him?" The oversize hulk with the nasty temper and the bulk to back it up? The barroom brawler with hands the size of canned hams? The person most likely to get riled if he saw another man in bed with his wife? Oh, yeah — that husband.

Jaylee dropped her panty hose and sat down on the edge of the bed. Her face turned whiter than the sheet she was sitting on. "Oh, my God. What if it was Carl, Robbie? He'll kill both of us as sure as the day is long, and he won't think nothing of it, either."

"That's just goddamn dandy, Jaylee." He began to pace back and forth, getting more angry with each step. "You might have told me you were married the first night you climbed into bed. You might have mentioned the fact that your husband rips heads off kittens for fun and breaks noses with his pinkie."

"I told you I was married!"

"About a day too late, wouldn't you say? Now what the hell am I supposed to do? Go invite Carl in for a drink and talk about the weather until he gets bored and decides to mash me into wood pulp?"

"What about me? If that was Carl at the window, he's going to hang around in the dark until he can get his paws on me. I want you to know I don't take kindly to being mashed myself, Mr. Robbie Drake. You might think about me before you make your own funeral arrangements!"

"I'm sorry, honeybee." He sat down beside her and offered her the bourbon bottle he discovered in one hand. "We got to think of something – and damned quick."

"We sure as hell do."

Carl Withers waited until the taillights winked in the distance, then awkwardly limped across the highway. There the forest was even darker, if such a thing was possible, and teeming with low branches and curling vines covered with thorns. It was blacker than the inside of a cow, he thought in his ponderous way, and having to keep an eye out for smokies was making him jumpier than a goddamn basket of bullfrogs. For some reason he could not analyze, it was all Jaylee's fault that he was there, hurt and damn near freezing.

He hadn't tried to call her or anything, but she should have known he would be coming in her direction and found some way to help him. Picked him up, maybe, or left some warm clothes and a gun where he could find it. Stupid bitch hadn't helped one bit. He decided he wasn't about to take her with him when he went to Houston. Oh, he'd slap her around for being such a selfish slut, but she could spend the rest of her life in the mobile-home park, gossiping and whining like a snot-nosed kid.

Yeah, he'd get the payoff like he'd been promised, then head south for Houston. Find some Texas woman with big tits and a warm bed, then send Jaylee a friggin' postcard or something.

He gave up trying to think and walk at the same time. His twisted ankle hurt like hell and it was getting colder. It was, he figured, at least forty more miles to Maggody.

FIVE

Bright and early Monday morning I went to the high school to question the local talent. It's a bigger school than you might think, since kids are bused in from miles around in battered yellow death traps. Maggody District High School usually has a so-so football team, but it does well at basketball, mostly because the latter requires fewer players. I used to go to the games and scream myself hoarse for the Maggody Marauders. A big time on Friday nights.

I waited around the front office for a few minutes, watching the kids come in to whine about tardy slips and unexcused absences, then followed a no-nonsense rump into the shrine for a word with the principal. For some reason, he failed to appreciate the purpose of my mission and we wasted a good fifteen minutes arguing about the Constitution and the students' rights to protection under the law, *blah, blah, blah.* All that from a man who strip searches female students in his office, with the door locked and the venetian blinds closed. If I ever get a signed complaint, I'm going to hang his balls from the flagpole out front, whether or not he's attached to them — in either sense of the word.

I gave up and went down to the shop room to speak to Larry Joe Lambertino, who I hoped might be able to help me get past the petty tyrant. The room was about the size of Carlsbad Caverns but jammed full of screaming table saws; rusted, skeletal cars on blocks; sweaty but dedicated welders; and a goodly amount of what appeared to be straightforward garbage. It smelled worse than the poultry processing factory in Starley City, if you can imagine. I never took shop myself; the reasons flooded back like a stopped-up toilet.

Things quieted down real quick when I entered the room. "Hey, Larry Joe," I called, so those with guilty consciences (about 80 percent, I estimated) would realize I hadn't come to arrest any of them — in the immediate future, anyway. "I need a little assistance from the town council."

Larry Joe jumped to his feet like he'd snuggled down on a hornet. "What do you want,

Arly? I'm real busy right now with the Shop II class; they're getting ready to tear down that Oldsmobile and I have to be there to supervise the winch. Then I got a advanced –"

"It'll only take a minute," I said, wondering why I was so all-fired popular these days. He could have smiled and offered me a seat, but he was watching me as if I had a bullsnake draped around my neck. I gave him a very brief account of the case of the kidnapped bureaucrat, which he didn't seem to enjoy a whole lot, and asked him to give me the names of any girls who might have been open (thighed) for business along the highway Friday morning.

"You think this guy from Dallas picked up one of the Maggody girls?" he asked. There was no denying the man was bright.

"I doubt it, but I thought I'd better ask around. The state boys are on my back about it, since the man was last seen at the Kwik-Screw and might have decided on a licentious interlude after he left."

"What'd Jim Bob say?"

"Jim Bob said he was going to apply his foot to my fanny. I presumed you'd heard about that last night at the Maggody Mafia meeting."

"At the what?" He didn't enjoy that, either. I thought it was kind of cute . . . the alliteration, you know, if nothing else. Try it a few times under your breath.

"I saw the cars parked behind Roy's when I went home last night," I said patiently. "If your wife thinks you were at prayer meeting, that's fine with me. You all are entitled to have your secret meetings; my lips are sealed tighter than a storm door and to hell with the Freedom of Information Act. Our town reporter hasn't made a meeting in six months, anyway; she makes up all the articles about the meetings based on what Jim Bob tells her the next day."

"We weren't talking about you last night. We were talking about something else completely unrelated."

"Gee, that's good to know, Larry Joe. I stayed up all night worrying about it, and you've eased my mind now. But I need to find out about any of the girls who might have been absent from school Friday, but not too sick to wiggle into jeans and take a ride down a back road."

"Are you sure you ought to get involved with this case, Arly? Why don't you let the state boys find that fellow while you worry about local matters?"

"The girls are local, and one of them may have gotten herself in trouble. Why don't you just tell me what I need to know and let me get out of here before I feel obliged to arrest somebody for something — like obstructing justice?" Sounded good, didn't it? Too bad it didn't mean anything, but it was enough to fool Larry Joe.

He gulped like he'd choked on two bugs and a locust. "How the heck am I supposed to know what some girl did Friday?"

"Why don't you ask the experts?"

Larry Joe beckoned to a group of pimply welders. They straggled over, as leery as a litter of undernourished field mice, and hemmed and hawed around until I offered a lame explanation about needing a witness for an accident. The thought of gore perked them up. After an enlightening discussion about the whereabouts of certain young ladies Friday morning (the boiler room, the boys' showers, and the parking lot were mentioned), they decided that none of the prime candidates had missed school. I asked if anyone had been out to the logging trail lately and received embarrassed denials and a goodly number of suggestive leers. From a bunch of fifteen-year-olds, for God's sake. I thanked them kindly and left.

Officer Buchanon was parked in the shade, keeping one eye on the signal light and the other on a toxicology manual. I pointed out that he wasn't on duty and he agreed, one of our standard conversations. I then told him the wenches were accounted for during the time in question and that I thought I'd work on the report for Sergeant Plover. When pressed, I also admitted I didn't know any of the seven deadly signs of cyanide and meekly listened to them, in descending order.

"I think I'll hear something today," Paulie said, as I started to drive away. "A deputy in Hasty who interviewed the same day as me heard in Saturday's mail. Jaylee and I can leave this hole together; I know I can convince her to divorce Carl once we get to Little Rock."

"Have you suggested that to her?"

"Not yet," he said, staring past my ear for a moment. "I'm so darn excited I don't know what to do. Can't you just picture me in a khaki trooper's uniform, right down to the wide-brimmed hat and the mirror sunglasses? Maybe I'll be assigned to Stump County so's we can still work together on an occasional case, Chief." He gave me a comradely wink, then gave himself one in the rearview mirror for practice.

"You'd better get accepted before you start giving me orders," I said, smiling.

"You think I won't get in?"

"You admitted yourself that the tests and interviews were tough, and even if you passed there's an overflow of applications every year.

You can always apply to the police academy if this doesn't work out." I had no idea about his chances with the state police, but he was beaming like a kid with a new two-wheeler. I hated the thought he might get hurt. I don't even step on spiders unless I have to.

"I don't want to go to the regular police academy. I'm going to the state police academy." Now he was frowning like he'd found a flat tire.

I waved and went on my way, full of sad thoughts about Paulie Buchanon. He still lived with his parents, who owned and operated the Pot O'Gold Mobile Home Park, where half the town lived in metal crates with wall-to-wall shag and all the modern conveniences except privacy and security from unscheduled flights to Oz. I suspected Paulie had been a shade too bright in school to be popular, a shade too small to be a jock, and way too sensitive to accept reality and make the best of it. He and Jaylee had been in the same class; he once told me he'd had a crush on her since second grade, when she let him peek at her panties during show-and-tell. Like jug wine, Jaylee had aged more rapidly, ending up with Carl. After Carl had been sent downstate to do time, Paulie tried to rekindle the relationship, but I suspected it remained on a second-grade level. No stolen kisses on the playground that I'd heard about, much less middle-school gropes.

Roy Stivers was standing in front of the PD when I got there. He was looking downright grizzled in his overalls and cap, his belly swelled out like he expected a bundle from heaven any day. He did not look capable of a sonnet or even a dirty limerick, but I knew better.

"Hey, Arly, I need to talk to you," he said, holding the screen door for me. Lord Byron would have done the same.

I poured us both some coffee and settled behind my desk. A snooty psychologist might read something in my taking refuge there in any storm, but I did prefer my string-bare leather seat and quick access to my duck.

"Whatcha need to talk about?" I asked. "You're not going to raise my rent, are you? God knows I'm paying too much already." About one-zillionth of what a New York apartment cost.

He slurped down some coffee, carefully not looking at me over the rim of the cup. "Nothing like that."

I was beginning to think I was a hands-down candidate for Miss Detestable of Maggody. Paulie liked me, sure, but not one other blessed soul in the whole goddamn town had bothered to smile at me for what seemed like a goddamn eternity. Roy was usually friendly; as I said earlier, I'd even been invited to swig bourbon in front of the stove and talk poetry with him.

"It's town business," he went on in a squirmy, apologetic voice. "Jim Bob's real pissed at you, Arly. He squawked about some incident up at his house and said you were belligerent and rude. He also mentioned your contract."

"Which runs another four months. Did he mention that I was at his house on official business, trying to cooperate with the state police on a case, or did he just talk about his threat to engage in assault and grievous bodily injury?"

Roy looked at me as if he'd discovered I wasn't depression glass after all; I was strictly plastic. I was getting used to it by now, so I grinned back and – you guessed it – took out my duck to consider how best to start on its webby little feet.

"What's that?" he asked, his brow in a cable-stitch.

"It's going to be a marshland mallard, but I just began on it."

"It don't look like a duck to me."

Did everyone nourish an art critic somewhere in his soul? "Listen, Roy, I have to write a report for the state boys about this fool bureaucrat who's probably living it up in the Tenderloin Hotel in Starley City, so I'd better get busy. If you came to warn me off Jim Bob, the message is received. If you came to tell me I've been canned, do it before I start the report and save me some sweat."

"Aw, Arly, don't start scratching like a dog with a load of fleas. I just think you ought to stay away from Jim Bob for a few days until both of you have a chance to calm down. Deer season starts pretty soon, and he won't have time to worry about firing you or finding a replacement with credentials."

"He'll be too occupied killing Bambi to bother with little old me, I suppose? I've got to write a report, Roy. Thanks for coming by to warn me, but I'm not going to let that fart scare me into hiding in the back of the barn for the next week."

"You'd better let the state boys look for the EPA fellow."

"Are you suggesting I engage in dereliction of duty? Oh, Roy, I am wounded to the bottom of my heart. Rest assured I am personally going to beat every bush in town for the man, since I suspect foul play." I didn't, but it sounded like television cop show dialogue, which is where I pick up my better lines.

"Your funeral, Arly. Heard anything about Carl Withers?"

I shook my head.

"What about Raz's bitch?" When I again shook my head, he told me I made real fine coffee and left me to write out a laborious description of all the things I hadn't discovered about the Dallas dude's brief encounter in Maggody. It wasn't exactly purple prose, but I made sure I spelled everything right before I ran it over to the state police headquarters in Farberville. I thought I might hand it over in person to Sergeant Plover, but I was informed rather officiously that said officer was unavailable at the moment and to leave the report in the box.

That delighted me so much that I hung around the edge of Farberville for most of an hour, watching tractor trailers refuel at a truck stop, and when the excitement got to be too much for me, had lunch at Suzie's Sunnyburgers. On the outside, it had a promising look, as if it were some little jewel of a culinary discovery that I could write home about. The Sunnyburger proved to be made of government-inspected, grade-A cow patty. Despite the ensuing grumbles from my stomach, I stopped at a classy bookstore in an old train station for a couple of paperback thrillers, windowshopped like a giggly teenaged girl, and generally wasted as much time as possible in the dereliction of duty.

When I got back to Maggody, I stopped at my apartment for a slug of milk of magnesia, then checked in with Officer Buchanon at the PD. He was sitting in my chair, but he looked so damn miserable I didn't have the heart to order him up. Duck or no duck, I still had a soul.

"Read this." He shoved a letter across the desk.

I already knew what it was going to say. I raised an eyebrow at the top line ("Buck Buchanon") but didn't say anything until I reached the bottom line, which wished him luck in future endeavors. It did not suggest he reapply to the state police academy.

It called for commiseration. "Officer Buchanon, I'm really sorry. Come on, I'll buy you a beer at Ruby Bee's and let you cry on my shoulder. Come hell or high water, you still have a job here and you can always try the regular police academy in Camden."

He did not appreciate my words of wisdom. After letting the black cloud above him settle more firmly on his head, he managed a grim smile. "I'm not interested in the regular police academy in Camden or a beer at Ruby Bee's.

You know I'm on duty, Chief. I'm not allowed to drink."

"I won't tattletale on you, and one beer won't hurt."

"You go ahead. I'm going to go run a speed trap the rest of the night, until I get so tired I can't read the numbers on the radar gun anymore. No one is going to make it through Maggody tonight at more than thirty miles per hour. Thirty-one and I'm going to bust the shit out of them."

I felt real bad for Paulie, but I could see he was going to vent his anger on motorists, which seemed constructive – and might pad the payroll. The idea of a beer sounded good, even alone, so I wished him luck with the unwary and went down the road to Ruby Bee's Bar and Grill.

Somebody with a peculiar sense of humor had replaced all the lightbulbs in the joint with pink ones. Pink crepe paper streamers were looped all over the ceiling, and clusters of balloons were taped on every available surface. The jukebox was blaring some happy honky-tonk about sex in the afternoon. Lots of folks were clumped in the middle of the room, whooping it up like it was New Year's Eve.

Naturally, I hadn't been invited, so I slipped in a booth and prepared to starve to death or to fall on the floor with ptomaine poisoning from Suzie's Sunnyburger (if you need to know, it had a strip of Velveeta cheese on it). Long about morning someone might find my body. Maybe the custodian, in a drunken daze, would sweep me out with the crepe paper and busted balloons. My mother would find me in a garbage can, deader than a squashed cootie.

I ducked at a loud pop, which I finally realized came from a champagne bottle rather than from an invisible sniper. Jaylee came prancing out of the mob, a glass held above her head like a trophy.

"Arly, honey!" she gushed when she spotted me. Old Faithful couldn't do it any better. "I'm enchanted that you came to celebrate with me, and real flattered. Get yourself a glass of bubbly!"

"Thanks, Jaylee, but my stomach can't face champagne at the moment. What are we celebrating?"

"You are looking at the next graduate of the Purley Institute of Hair Design and Beauty. I passed the GED; I'm on my way to Little Rock and even bigger places, Arly. Why, I could end up in Dallas or Los Angeles or some place like that, working for Vidal Sassoon hisself!"

Vidal was no doubt swooning in his Manhattan penthouse. "That's great news," I said, forcing a smile. "Did you hear that Paulie received a letter from the state police admissions office?"

"Oh, my God." She sank down across from me and tossed off the champagne. "You don't sound like he heard good news. Aw, pee in the bathtub, Arly, he was so sure he'd get in. I sort of promised we could spend some time together down in Little Rock, especially since I won't know anybody myself and at least I'd recognize his ugly mug. We was even talking about having dinner in a real high-class place for his birthday next month. How's he taking it?"

"He's upset. I suggested he apply to the regular academy, and he almost bit my head off. I don't know what to do about him, except maybe stay out of his sight for the next few months."

"And I'm leaving just when he's down in the dumps!" She twisted her hands and chewed off a few centimeters of lipstick, trying to pretend she was seriously considering not making a beeline for the Purley Institute and Vidal hisself. "I feel terrible. What'd you think I ought to do, Arly?"

"Do what you think you have to do," I said, refusing to be helpful in her hour of crisis. "Good luck and all that, Jaylee. You did real fine to pass the GED, and you deserve to celebrate. When are you leaving town?"

"After the party. I plan to run back to my mobile home and pack, then throw everything in the car and make tracks faster than a coon in heat. You – ah, you heard any word on Carl?"

"He was seen in Arkadelphia, but the report hadn't been confirmed last time I checked. Is Carl the reason you're so eager to leave town so quickly?"

"He's not as bad as everybody thinks, you know." She let out a bubbly sigh and stared at the table. "When he got arrested for DWI, auto theft, and leaving-the-scene, I was just floored. He'd been sick to his stomach for a couple days and had been on the couch watching television all that evening with not more than one six-pack of Bud. He all of a sudden got a bug up his ass and drove off with some excuse about needing another six-pack. There wasn't any reason for him to steal that Eldorado and go joyriding, not on one six-pack. He didn't even sweat over a case. It must have been on account of the tart that called right before he decided he needed more beer."

"But he was alone when they finally chased him down, wasn't he?"

"Nobody ever said otherwise, so I guess he was."

"Did you find out the name of the woman involved?"

"I wasn't all that fired up about the idea of him screwing someone else, but I didn't much care. It usually held down the wear and tear on yours truly, if you get what I mean. Anyway, an hour later I got the call from the sheriff's office, telling me what bad-ass trouble Carl was in. I offered the next morning to tell the sheriff that he couldn't have been drunk, but he got mad and started cussing at me, so I decided he could rot in prison for all I cared."

"He confessed, didn't he?"

She nodded, her eyes still aimed at the table. "It was real puzzling, but I don't reckon it matters now. They're going to be pretty pissed about him escaping."

As I shrugged, Ruby Bee and Estelle came out of the kitchen with a big, drippy banner made out of white muslin and poster paint. The red letters wished Jaylee *Best of Luck in the Big City*. The crowd *oohed* appreciatively while the two paraded around the room and finally stopped at the jukebox to tape their artwork on the wall. I'd seen better stuff on refrigerators, but the sentiment was kind of sweet.

Jaylee burst into tears and rushed around the room to hug everyone, swearing she'd just die without them but they'd better come see her in Little Rock if they didn't want their asses whomped. Everybody assured her they would see her real soon, and it wasn't like she was moving to Alaska or something. She was headed for me, puckered up and teary, when she saw Paulie in the doorway. After the briefest flicker of hesitation, she veered straight for him.

"Oh, Paulie, honey," she said, swooping down like a barn owl, "I heard about your bad news! I just cried — I really did! I feel worse about it than I would if *I'd* failed the test again."

Paulie gave her a big smack and told her several times how happy he was for her. It was so touching we all got misty and had to bury our noses in our beers and slurp around for a few minutes. The only flaw in all this emotionalism was that Ruby Bee and Estelle stayed across the room, as far away from me as possible, and stared as if I had recently arisen from a grave. Whispers, dark looks, the whole welcome wagon bit I'd gotten used to in the last few days. To top it off, Jim Bob showed up with Mrs. Jim Bob, kissed Jaylee right on the lips, and announced he was buying. He then joined Ruby Bee and Estelle, making a total of six cold eyes aimed in my direction. Or five, anyway. One of Estelle's wanders.

The idea of a free round set everybody off with the whoops and kisses. A couple of quarters in the jukebox, bottles of beer, pink lights, and Maggody was practically some New York disco. I sat and grinned for most of an hour, pretending I was having a great time in the back booth by myself. Whoop-de-do.

At one point, nature being what it is, I shoved through the crowd for a visit to the ladies' room. As I waited by the door, I heard voices from the hall beside the kitchen — Jaylee in conversation with my favorite person, His Honor the Moron. I couldn't get much of it over the blare from the jukebox, but it sounded angry. Trouble appeals to the cop in me, so I stuck my head around the corner and waved. "Hey, y'all smooching behind Mrs. Jim Bob's back?"

Jim Bob jumped higher than a bobwhite. "You're fired, Ariel Hanks! Turn in your badge before I rip it off your — your uniform! I have just about had it with you and I want you to —"

Jaylee put her hand over his mouth. "You leave Arly alone, honeybunch . . . unless you want to explain to your wife why we're back here having our little talk. Now I'll see you later like we said."

He was still bulging his eyeballs at me, so I returned to the business at hand. While I was on the pot, I tried to decide what any of it meant. Jim Bob having an affair with Jaylee — possible; him mad she was leaving — possible; totally uninteresting — definitely. I spent the last few minutes reading a sign Ruby Bee had taped on the inside of the stall door: *Please don't sprinkle when you tinkle.* I'd never realized my mother was a closet poetess with a real feel for delicate sentiment. Jim Bob and Jaylee were gone when I came out.

I whooped it up for a while, then my whooper got tired so I decided to go home. I doubted that my departure was going to break up the party, but you never knew.

Robert listened to the din in the distance, hating it more with each passing second. The stupid bitch was in there, he figured, letting everybody know she was the newest Einstein now that she had her crummy little high-school diploma. He was ready to split as soon as she could drag herself away and get her ass packed. His clothes had been packed since his dinner tray had been delivered by some weird broad with red hair. Beans and cornbread — and he was supposed to be grateful.

He looked at the curtain closed tightly across the window. There was maybe just a hairline crack, but he figured only some Cyclops could see through it. Carl was reputed to have two eyes, if one hadn't been poked out in some prison brawl. Carl, who'd seen them in bed and was likely to rip out a few eyes himself.

He really wanted her to come, quickly. Hell, it was dark now, and it was time to get out of the dump and back to civilization. Even back to Dawn Alice, if he had to, and her yuppie tennis pro with the molded calves and pearly white teeth glinting against a bottled tan.

Robert paced for a while, sat down on the bed to drink for a while, and finally lay back against the pillow to listen to the thumpety-thump of his heart. It seemed to match the rhythm of the music streaming out of Ruby Bee's Bar and Grill into the cold night air.

Carl Withers moved along the creek bank, doing his damnedest not to slip and fall into the water, which he knew was mighty cold in October. His ankle had swelled bigger than a baseball bat and was burning like it was on fire. Raz's house was dark; his dog pen silent. Lucky, but shit — he figured he deserved a little luck after four days in the woods. Redskins might like to eat roots and berries, but he'd decided the day before that they weren't worth the trouble of finding and picking. Something had done bad service to his stomach already, and he was still a touch queasy when he remembered.

He crossed Finger Lane and headed for the pay telephone in the shadows next to the laundromat. His last dime, but just as good as one of those fancy blue chips. The thought warmed him like a tiny match. First the payoff, then a surprise visit with Jaylee. He'd have a thousand bucks in his pocket by then, and he could head south as soon as he was finished beating on her. But it was, he reckoned after a long halt to count on his fingers, pretty damn close to deer season. It'd be a damn shame to leave without killing something.

Jim Bob excused himself from the ladies and went to telephone Roy. After a growl of identification, he told Roy to call the other council members quick and have everybody meet him outside Ruby Bee's. He was on his second cigar when they finally arrived, and his mood had not improved.

"Arly's on to something," he muttered. "Ruby Bee and Estelle say she keeps hanging around, asking funny questions and pretending she's not suspicious."

Larry Joe and Roy nodded as Ho took the floor. "This was all your idea, Jim Bob. You said this was the only way to save the creek, and all we had to do was keep the fellow entertained until Fiff got back from Las Vegas. I don't have no problem with a brief delay, but I ain't about to get myself involved in a kidnap charge." He ran his fingers through his hair, not even caring what damage he did. A nerve jumped along his eyelid like a flea in the upholstery. "I got to think about my reputation in the county, as well —"

"Shut up." Jim Bob threw his cigar into the darkness. "I think we're still safe, but you just remember we're all in this together, like the goddamn musketeers. Arly isn't going to arrest her mother, for Christ's sake."

Larry Joe began to bobble. "I don't know, Jim Bob; she was real crusty today at school."

"She told me she was going to get to the bottom of this," Roy contributed in an unhappy voice, his face lost in the shadows. "She's likely to arrest all of us, her mother and Estelle included, and throw us to the state boys. They won't feel so kindly about this so-called delay."

"What the fuck do you want me to do about it?" Jim Bob snarled. "You three boys are acting like the preacher caught you with a toad in your pocket on Communion Sunday. We've gone too far to let the fellow waltz out of here and head for the state police. We got to think of a way to keep him happy a little longer, and we can't keep him at the Flamingo. If we don't get support from Fiff, your asses are going to be on the line right next to mine."

Roy stared at the light streaming through the window. "I got an idea, Jim Bob. Let's take Drake up to the deer camp. Arly'll never think to look for him there, and he sure isn't going to walk away and make a phone call from some pine tree."

There was a long silence while the others considered it. At last Jim Bob spat out a flake of cigar skin and slapped Roy on the shoulder. "That'll work — at least for a day or two. I'll tell the little woman we decided to go up early to scout and have her pack a box of food. Meet you all here in an hour." He started to leave, then stopped and spun around. "Let's go ahead and get him now, before something happens and the shit hits the fan. I can think of the perfect place to put Mr. Drake so we won't have to worry."

Jaylee hummed as she folded her clothes into tidy packages and put them in the suitcase. The party had been almost as good as her sixteenth birthday party, and a lot more fun at the end. For a while, she'd thought it would go on all night, with everyone just kissing and hugging her and wishing her luck in the future. She realized she was humming "Happy Birthday," but why not? It was kinda like a birthday, all shimmery and full of hope.

She slammed the lid shut, glanced around one final time to make sure the mobile home was in apple-pie order, and grabbed her suitcase. After a peek out the door in case Carl was around (she'd thought she heard him earlier — and damn near wet her pants), she hurried to her car and put the suitcase in the backseat. Robbie was going to be mad 'cause she was late, but she'd make it up to him when they stopped at a hotel. Maybe they could drive all the way to Little Rock and stay in some grand place with twenty stories and a restaurant on the tippy top. They could eat those skinny French pancakes with sauce all over them, and a sprig of parsley right on the plate for color. Why not — she could afford it now, couldn't she? She patted her purse on the seat beside her and allowed a flicker of satisfaction. It had looked bad for a moment, like she was going to have to call their bluff, but then she'd been saved by the second visitor. Saved and paid.

"Bye-bye, Pot O'Gold," she trilled as she drove through the gate for the last time. It had lived up to its name, for her anyway, even if she'd worked hard for the money. She called farewells to each house, barn, and building she passed along the highway, and even waved at Paulie in his cruiser by the signal light, although he seemed to be reading one of his eternal police books and didn't even see her. It really was a shame about him, she thought, allowing a brief sigh before returning to her more cheerful frame of mind. She turned in at the faded sign that promised blue-plate specials at Ruby Bee's. Well, she wouldn't miss Maggody, but she'd sort of miss Ruby Bee and Estelle; they'd been loyal friends for a long time and real encouraging every time she'd failed the GED and sat at the bar and cried her eyes out like some damn fool kid. She'd miss Arly, too; it'd been right tough having to snub her to keep her away from the bar — and the motel.

She parked in front of Number Three, just like Robbie had told her to a thousand times. After a furtive glance around the parking lot, she scurried to the door, unlocked it with trembling hands, and slipped inside.

It was vacant. Empty. Unoccupied. Not a rat's ass sign of Mr. Robbie Baby Drake.

Jaylee swallowed an unladylike comment and went back to the door, her mouth screwed up with righteous anger. She threw the door open and squinted into the darkness.

"You out there hiding, Robbie baby? Is this

some kind of game to get back at me for being late?"

There was a twitch of movement in the shadows, nothing you could put your finger on, just a twitch.

"Is that you?" Jaylee said, suddenly afraid.

The pain came from nowhere. It exploded in her throat, threw her against the half-open door, turned white and pink and purple at the same time like a crazy kaleidoscope show and a birthday party rolled into one. And red, so very red. She was thinking it was sorta pretty as she slid to the ground to die.

S I X

Maggody had been on the move earlier, but things quieted down long about eleven o'clock.

Larry Joe and Roy arrived first at the deer camp, bleary from the beer and painfully conscious of the condition of their bladders. They took the boxes and sleeping bags out of the trunk and began to lug them inside, where it would be warm once they got the propane heater lit. It was getting damn cold, they agreed as they crossed paths in the weedy clearing.

The second car came after a bit, delayed by the necessity of crawling along the ruts so as not to punch holes in the oil pan. The passenger in the back continued a steady stream of invectives. Jim Bob and Ho had quit paying much attention to him about the time they turned off the highway, not that they'd minded the cussing. It was almost instructive, the vocabulary being on a higher plane than they were used to. Some of it was real colorful.

There weren't many lights burning in downtown Maggody, except for the streetlight in front of the post office and the light in the office of the middle school. The apartment above the antique shop was dark, as was the neon sign in front of Ruby Bee's. A light in there suddenly went off, and the sound of a door being closed was followed by boozy female murmurs drifting into the parking lot. A nightcap was suggested in a naughty whisper.

The Flamingo Inn sign was on, of course, in perpetual optimism that some leaden-eyed tourist would see the *V can y* sign and read it as a message from heaven, the means to salvation from falling asleep at the wheel and ending up in a ditch somewhere. A pink neon silhouette of a peg-legged flamingo glittered below the words, in case someone couldn't read too well. Behind the motel there was no light, just a smooth expanse of motionless darkness like an inland sea of ink. Jaylee's body lay undisturbed in the doorway of Number Three.

There was a yellow bulb beside the front door of the PD, and a light on inside. Through the venetian blinds you could see a sad young man at the desk, a textbook clutched in two white fists as if he could absorb the material through brute physical contact. His eyes were red, but his lips continued to move as he read the emergency treatment for the inhalation of sulfur gas.

In a small glow of light from a candle on the floor, the man with the swollen ankle wolfed down sandwiches as fast as he could, despite the fire snakes that darted up his leg. He was thinking about the thousand dollars he didn't have, how he deserved it and was gonna get it. And somebody was gonna pay for every step of his trip, every minute he had spent in the goddamn freezing night. Gonna pay real bad.

The lights were ablaze in the Kwik-Stoppe-Shoppe, promising a veritable haven of warmth and creature comforts in an otherwise oblivious town. Shelves of overpriced products were bathed in the white light to appeal from the highway, if anyone slowed down long enough to admire the view. Dahlia unwrapped a chocolate bar and popped half of it in her mouth, then tossed the paper on the floor and gazed down into the little cavern under the counter. Oddly inflamed by her impassive face, Kevin gave her a shy smile before returning to his lesson.

There was a light on at the Voice of the Almighty Lord Assembly Hall, although it was hardly regular prayer-meeting time. The two kneeling figures didn't care; there was sin afoot in Maggody, and only immediate appeals to God could save the collective soul of the community from the clutches of Satan himself.

In a small house in Farberville, a bedroom light snapped on. A figure stumbled to the bathroom for a glass of water, then retraced his path back to bed, muttering all the time. She had to have a first name. Everybody had a first name. Nobody named an innocent baby Chief, unless it was some crazy Indian papa with grand ideas. Maybe he could get it from Camden, if he could think of a legitimate-sounding reason.

SEVEN

The telephone rang six or seven times before it wormed its way into my dream. I rolled across the bed and grabbed the damn thing, thinking of a few choice words for anyone dumb enough to wake me up in the middle of the night.

"Ariel! You got to get over here real quick!"

The only person who calls me Ariel is Ruby Bee. For the record, I was not named after the character from Shakespeare's *Tempest;* I was named after a photograph of Maggody taken from an airplane. Ruby Bee, not exactly a champion speller, has a copy of it in her bedroom, the bar and motel outlined in ink. The Hanks clan is notorious for whimsy when naming innocent babies — Ruby Bee is a nickname for Rubella Belinda. Everybody agreed it had a fine ring to it.

"What time is it?" I growled.

122

"I don't know — just get over here!"

"I'm not moving until you tell me what time it is and why I'm supposed to 'get over here,' " I said through a yawn. I might have sounded a mite peevish by this point.

"It's right about three, I'm at the motel and—" She made a gurgly noise, like she was trying not to break down or throw up. "It's Jaylee, Ariel. She's dead."

I sat up, switched on the lamp, and stared at the receiver. "She's dead? What are you talking about? Jaylee told me she was leaving town after the party."

"She never made it. Her body's on the ground in front of Number Three, and you'd better get over here and do something."

I promised to be there in a couple of minutes. I threw on some clothes, called the sheriff's department, grabbed my gun, and ran down the stairs, too shocked to try to figure out what the hell was going on or what Jaylee was doing at the Flamingo Inn when she should have been a hundred miles along the road to success.

After a drive down the center of the highway at seventy miles per hour, I squealed into the parking lot, tore around back, and slammed on the brakes in a spray of gravel and dust, just as Bullitt would have done. I hadn't bothered with the bubble light, since not a creature was stirring in Maggody at such an ugly hour.

Estelle and Ruby Bee were standing under the porch light in front of Number One. The dull light made them look eerie, as if they were characters in some voodoo melodrama off-off-Broadway. I gaped at the heap in the doorway of Number Three, then joined them on the porch.

"Are you sure she's dead?" I asked in a low voice.

"I'm sure," Ruby Bee said. "Her eyes were wide open and staring at nothing I could see. She has a funny, surprised look on her face, but she sort of looks like she's smiling." She shivered, then said, "There's a lot of blood, Ariel — her neck was busted open and it must have spewed out for a long time."

I knew I was supposed to hold the scene until the sheriff's boys arrived, but there wasn't a soul in sight except the three of us, so I left the tape and stakes in the trunk of my car. The rubberneckers would come in hordes the next day; for the moment they were all in their beds. Praise the Lord and pass up the police procedure.

"You'd better go look," Estelle said. She and Ruby Bee exchanged the guarded looks I had learned to expect, and seemed to arrive at an understanding. "We got to tell you something afterwards."

I doled out a pair of scowls, then went across the gravel to do a quick examination of the body. Ruby Bee was right about the smile on Jaylee's face — and the blood. I squatted down and studied the splattered flesh that had been her neck before someone put a four-inch hole in it. She couldn't have survived for more than a few seconds, but it had been long enough to let her heart pump out most of the blood in her body.

There was no weapon to be seen. I was pretty sure I knew what had made the wound (a mild word for such violence), but I decided to let the medical examiner make the formal announcement. Anyone who grows up in a place where all males over the age of eight hunt learns to recognize the methodology of death. A crossbow arrow this time. As deadly as a bullet and as silent as snow, except for one tiny twang. Even if she'd heard it, there wouldn't have been time to duck.

Blue lights started flashing all over the place. Doors slammed, men barked at each other, radios crackled and popped, boots crunched across the gravel. Puffs of vapor rose from mouths as if they internalized cigarettes.

Robert Drake was not delighted with his new

accommodations. The rusty silver trailer didn't have any plumbing he could find, and it smelled like a wet dog had puked daily in it for a solid month. The furniture in the motel hadn't been any great shakes, but this stuff was horrible. The bed was lumpy, the dresser right out of a damaged-freight sale, the walls painted a nauseating shade of green that matched his mood. The carpet was matted so badly it didn't have a color.

He got off the bed (ha!) and went to the door of the room, which took all of two steps. His captors still hunkered around a dinette table, with untidy piles of plastic poker chips between the beer cans and overflowing ashtrays. The room was thick with a blue cloud of smoke from cheap cigars. The goddamn poker game had been going on for hours. Robert had played for a time, but they'd fleeced him without mercy and he didn't like to lose.

"How long are you going to keep me here?" he demanded from the doorway.

Jim Bob glanced up. "Nobody's keeping you, Drake. You can head out anytime you want. Be sure and send us a postcard if you think about it." He turned back to the game. "Now, Roy, if I honestly believed you had another lady in the hole, I'd have to fold and let you rake in them pretty chips. But a little birdie keeps whispering in my ear that you ain't got horsefeathers in the hole, so I think I'll see your raise and add another ten to sweeten the pot."

"Your ten, and ten more," Roy said, leaning back with a smug look. Larry Joe dropped his cards on the table and reached into an ice chest for another beer. Ho belched in surprise and folded.

"Read 'em and weep," Jim Bob said as he spread his cards.

"Goddamn it!" Robert went back into the tiny room and flopped across the bed. "Nobody's keeping you, Drake," he said in a bitter voice. "You can head out anytime you want to, and remember to send us a goddamn postcard! Just send it care of Smokey the Bear."

First, they'd come for him like a gang of storm troopers, marched him out the door, and forced him to climb into the trunk of a Cadillac. It had been what felt like hours before anybody had thought to see if he'd suffocated. Goddamn clowns deserved a murder rap. He'd been afraid they'd leave him there, in the stinking coffin, but they finally decided to put him in the back seat of some four-wheel crate that was almost worse than the Caddie trunk, if you breathed deeply.

He'd been blindfolded during the drive, but he could tell they were at least twenty miles into nowhere; the last few miles had been on a road so rough he'd almost lost his dinner. He glared through the narrow window at the blackness outside. The shitheels in the other room would get a real kick out of him trying to escape in that pitch-black crap. They knew, as did he, that he'd make it about five feet from the trailer, then fall down and break a leg — or run into some sort of bear or mountain lion and end up as a midnight snack. He had no idea which way to go. No flashlight, no heavy shoes, or even a warm coat. There wasn't any way to stroll out of the mess he was in. What he needed, he thought with a sly smile, was a set of car keys.

He went back into the other room and sat down at the table. "Deal me in. I trust you gentlemen'll take a check."

I was questioned about the identity and other vitals of the body and allowed to admit I had no idea what had happened in the doorway of Number Three. After I was instructed to remain available, I was ignored for a long time while the county men did the mundane details. The county coroner arrived after an hour, puffing and wheezing about being routed from bed in the middle of the night just so he could tell them what any damn fool could see in one glance. The ambulance came and left with a delivery for the morgue. One deputy did a fair outline in chalk of the blood splatters that had turned to dirty brown on the walk, the wall, the door, and the edge of the gravel. Everybody agreed there was a lot of blood.

Sergeant Plover arrived toward sunrise, looking as gray as the cold mushy fog he'd brought with him. He didn't even wave before he joined the big boys for a long, low talk, which I thought was less than polite, considering our history. After a lot of talk, things settled down and the carnival began to pack up and drift away.

At some point Ruby Bee and Estelle had drifted away, too. We hadn't had our cozy little chat yet, and I found myself hoping we could have it over coffee hot enough to stop my shivers. I was eyeing the back of the bar for signs of life or smells of coffee when Plover deigned to acknowledge my insignificant presence.

"Where's the woman who found the body?"

"Making coffee, I hope. And how are you this lovely October morning, Sergeant Plover?"

He scratched his cheek, which was sprouting stubbles before my eyes. You would have thought he could have wasted a few seconds with a razor before heading into the limelight.

He gave me a slow study and drawled, "I'm fine, Chief Hanks. How are you?"

"Fine, thank you." I rewarded him with a smile and started for the kitchen door.

"Wait a minute," he said, actually touching my jacket. "You haven't given me a report yet, or told me where to find the witness. This isn't the time for childish tantrums, Chief." He hit the last word hard, as if it were an insult. I'd always liked the word, but I flinched at his tone.

"It is the time for coffee, however, so that's where I'm going. I'll tell you what I know while I thaw and then introduce you to the witness, who is also my mother."

Ruby Bee had indeed made coffee; it smelled so good I would have fainted if Sergeant Plover hadn't been stepping on my heels. Estelle was slumped over the bar, her head supported by her fists. Her eyes were redder than bing cherries and her face streaked with black snail tracks of mascara. Ruby Bee looked just as bad as she came out of the kitchen with a tray of cups and saucers. Someone had cast a shadow on the sunshine girls.

I introduced everybody to everybody else and crawled into the coffee. Sergeant Plover (maybe he didn't have a first name) asked Ruby Bee when she'd found Jaylee's body. It struck me as an innocent question, but Ruby Bee recoiled like he'd spit at her. Estelle just closed her eyes and let out a despondent sigh.

"I don't know exactly," Ruby Bee managed to say in a shaky voice. "We closed up about one, then stayed around more than an hour to pull down the crepe paper and bust the balloons. They was for Jaylee's party, and they looked real pretty . . . "

"Jaylee Withers, the victim," Plover said, nodding. "Why don't you pour me some coffee, then you and Miss Oppers can tell me all about the party?"

The two of them related the purpose and highlights of the party and, with prodding, the guest list as best they could remember. I was mentioned, which merited a raised eyebrow or two. I dumped a couple of teaspoons of sugar into the next cup of coffee, figuring I would need a little excess energy soon, then decided to be a good cop.

"She told me she was leaving town as soon as she could get away from the party," I volunteered. "That was about seven o'clock."

"Jaylee finally got away around a quarter after eight," Ruby Bee said. "She said she was going straight to her mobile home and expected to leave town as soon as she was packed. She gave me a real nice hug, like I was her mother, and promised to write." She hiccupped in her coffee cup, her shoulders hunched up tight with misery.

"We found her car parked behind the motel, loaded with suitcases and makeup paraphernalia. She had more than a thousand dollars in her purse. That blows robbery as a motive." Plover scratched his cheek for a while, then looked at me. "If she intended to pack and leave, why did she go to the motel?"

"I have no idea," I said brightly. "Let's ask our witnesses."

Our witnesses turned whiter than unblanched string beans in a Mason jar. They both began gabbling denials of any knowledge of anything at all, until Plover tired of it and raised his hand to stop them in mid-gab.

"Then why don't we leave that for later and move on to another fascinating question: Who was staying in Number Three?"

"Nobody," Ruby Bee gasped. "I haven't had anyone stay at the motel for more than a month, and then it was some kids from Starley City who wanted a place to drink beer and—"

"The room was occupied for several days, ma'am. We've been trained to look for evidence, and we couldn't miss this batch unless we'd kept our eyes closed and our noses pinched. A male Caucasian with dark hair and a propensity for lime aftershave and sexual activity, but we'll know more when we get the lab reports back."

I shoved the coffee cup aside so I could have better aim for my outraged stare. "Who was staying there?" I said slowly, each syllable enunciated with precision and great care.

Ruby Bee met my eyes for a second, then looked at the floor. "That EPA fellow. He came Friday afternoon."

"He came Friday afternoon," I echoed, incredulous. "You mean he just drove up and requested a room so he could disappear for four days? You didn't think to mention it to me?"

"He didn't exactly ask for a room," Estelle said. "He was sort of brought in, but he didn't object. Why, he was cracking jokes the entire time and acting like it was a Rotary luncheon."

"Sort of brought in? Who was this delivery boy?"

"The town council." Ruby Bee said it so low I almost didn't catch it, and it took several seconds for it to sink in. It finally did, and it landed like a jab of electricity from a frayed cord. Plover was just sitting there, letting me do the work while he made stealthy scribbles in his notebook.

I finally found my breath. "Let me see if I have this right. The town council, meaning Jim

Bob, Larry Joe, Roy, and Hobert, brought the EPA man to the motel and helped him check in for the weekend. Everybody thought it was so funny they acted like stand-up comedians, including the missing bureaucrat. Then one of the jokers politely drove the state car to the middle of the national forest and left it there, so that I'd waste time crawling around the blackberry thickets on my hands and knees to look for a corpse. That right so far, Ruby Bee?"

She nodded numbly. "Something like that. The man was maybe just a hair unhappy, and we did pick the unit with the deadbolt so he couldn't change his mind in the middle of the night."

"He had trays three times a day," Estelle contributed, "and a scandalous number of bottles of bourbon. It wasn't like he was in a dungeon or anything. The three of us took care of him right well."

I stopped to count, and it didn't take long. "Jaylee was providing entertainment, wasn't she? Bringing trays and sex to the man in Number Three? You two ought to be hung from the sign out front — by your little pink toes, you know that? You are unbelievable, you and the councilmen! What you did was a felony, not some cute prank to fool the police while Jaylee rolled around in bed with the kidnapped man!"

Ruby Bee gave me the old hand-in-the-cookie-jar look, all wide-eyed and wounded to fake penitence better. "Jim Bob said we had to save Boone Creek." *Sniff, sniff.* "He said it was the only way. Remember how you used to swim there every summer, Ariel? It was always so cool and peaceful to just drift along in the current, watching the clouds and dreaming about the future." *Sniff, sniff, sniff.* "That's partly why we were so nervous about you coming to the bar." *Sniff* again. "We were afraid you'd catch on to what we was doing."

"Felon!" I growled.

"Ariel?" Plover said.

"Three cowboys and a pair of ducks," Ho announced, placing his cards on the table with a flourish. "I won't embarrass you boys by allowing you to show your pitiful straights and flushes." Even as he raked in the chips, throwing out a few obligatory jeers along the way, he kept dwelling on his problem. He had the best reputation in the county, and it was real important to keep it. If his dealership dried up, he wouldn't be able to support his two children anymore, and they sure as hell couldn't last five minutes without him. His son was waiting tables in San Francisco; Ho didn't want to even guess at what the boy did when he wasn't prancing around in an apron. Mary Jane was married to a worthless son of a bitch who couldn't hold down a job from one hunting season to the next, and she'd let herself get impregnated again, just like goddamn clockwork. It was a blessing that their mother wasn't alive to see the wreckage the two had made of their lives.

Ho slammed a chip in the middle of the table. "Dollar to see the next card, boys."

Plover dragged the rest of the story out of them. Afterward, I banged down a dollar and stomped out the front door, my eyes burning and my head so sore it felt likely to explode. Plover caught me in the parking lot and told me to wait there, then went around back to see what was happening at the crime scene. Even though it had sounded like an order, I waited, mostly because I was too tired to stir up enough perversity to leave.

Paulie drove up while I was standing there. "Is it true?" he said, controlled but grim.

"It's true, and I'm sorry." I was going to add more, but I started shivering so hard my teeth rattled. Hell, I'd liked Jaylee. She'd had a rough time and had managed to drag herself out and to try to do something that was sensible, if not exactly earth-shattering or profound. Vidal would have liked her, too. I got in the car with Paulie and turned up the heater.

"I heard from the sheriff's office," Paulie said. "I couldn't believe it for a long time; I just sat there and thought how no one could take the life out of Jaylee. She was too happy, too excited, and eager to get out of this dump, too —" He broke off with a sob.

I patted his shoulder while he cried.

We were just sitting there when Plover came around the corner of the bar. He motioned for me to roll down the window, then said, "The sheriff has been in communication with my office, and we've decided to centralize the investigation here in Maggody. That means we'll use your office, Chief, and you'll be expected to give us full cooperation. I've already sent deputies to pick up the four council members and bring them in for questioning. The sheriff has agreed to call up his posse to search the woods for the EPA man, although he's probably long gone by now. You've got time to go home and freshen up, and I'll see you at your office in thirty minutes. Any questions?"

"Yeah, what's your first name?"

"Sergeant." He left, chuckling under his breath like some biddy on a nestful of eggs.

I told Paulie to drive me around to the back

so I could get my car. "Where've you been all night?" I asked.

"Giving tickets like I said I was going to do. Collected about a hundred in fines and two promises to get my ass kicked in municipal court, which is about average." He turned pink and added, "I turned the police band off so I could try to decide what to do, but I did stay awake. I went back to the PD about one A.M. and fooled around with the toxicology book, even though it isn't going to do me one damn bit of good. What happened to – to Jaylee?"

"I don't know yet, but I did learn some fascinating stuff about the occupancy of Number Three, which has some bearing on the case. You aren't going to believe your ears." I told him what I'd learned about the kidnappee and the kidnappers, which included an impressive roster of local dignitaries and the police chief's mother. He didn't believe me at first, but, hell – I wouldn't have either. I skipped the bit about Jaylee's undercover visits to Number Three, stressing that her only involvement was to take trays and magazines and return with dirty dishes.

"In the middle of the afternoon and late at night?" Paulie laughed, but not with a real deep humor. "The fellow was a hungry sumbitch, wasn't he?"

138

"We don't know why she was there, and Drake didn't hang around to explain. It looks bad for him. Maybe something happened between them, and he got frightened and killed her in a panic."

"Right, Chief. He was so scared he hurried right out to steal a crossbow, then loaded it and waited for her to show up in the doorway. Standard panicky procedure."

"Shit, I don't know, Officer Buchanon. It's only a couple of weeks to deer season; one of the Mafiosi might have brought a crossbow to the motel so the EPA fellow could look at it. In any case, it seems we're having company at the PD, and I forgot to put on a bra. Don't go home; I'm going to need you today."

I drove to the apartment and parked out front, thinking I'd drive back across the highway like a real cop. A state trooper stepped out of the shadows below the stairs, which I have to admit scared the piss out of me for a full three seconds.

He looked at my uniform, rumpled but there, and gave me a halfhearted salute. "You're the chief of police?"

"I live here, in the upstairs apartment. Did you come to fetch Roy for questioning?"

"I did, but he ain't here. His truck's gone, and nobody could sleep through the racket I made on the back door."

"Wait a minute." I went upstairs, brushed my teeth, tethered my breasts, and grabbed the key to Roy's store, given to me when I first moved in case I heard burglars making off with the porcelain pitchers. The deputy and I went inside and searched the back room, but Roy sure as hell wasn't there. His dresser drawers were empty.

He wasn't the only one who'd flown the coop. When I got to the station, I heard that the entire council was out for the night. And nobody seemed to know where they were. Mrs. Jim Bob and Mrs. Lambertino swore they didn't know anything. Ho and Roy didn't have anybody sharing their beds and available to tattle on them. The sheriff's dispatcher said the patrol had searched the area north of Boone Creek and were moving along the bank toward the national forest.

For Sergeant Plover's educational benefit, I ticked off the missing men on my fingers: Richard Drake, Jim Bob, Roy, Larry Joe, Hobert — and Carl Withers. You'd have thought Maggody was a black hole in the universe. Of course, I'd suspected as much since I was five years old.

EIGHT

Sergeant Plover thanked me for the nose count and asked if he might sit at my desk in order to use the telephone. I asked him where he expected me to sit, and he allowed that the PD was going to need some more furniture while it served as a crime room. We looked at each other for a long time, him grinning and me trying to decide what sort of first name he might have. Probably something stupid like Percival, I concluded. At least he'd found time to shave.

The sheriff's boys came in to confer about things too complicated for little old me, so I told them to get a table and chairs from Roy's store, tossed the key on the desk, and sailed out of there before the claustrophobia got a firm grip on me. One of the deputies stuck his head out the door before I reached my car.

141

"Sergeant Plover wants to know where you're going, ma'am."

A trick question. In the back of my mind, I was planning to go to Ruby Bee's for breakfast and issue some more outrage at the treachery and deceit visited on me for the last five days. I was then going to have a paddy wagon from a convent pick up Ruby Bee and Estelle, and drive them away to a place where they'd have to behave – the worst punishment I could concoct on an empty stomach and four hours of sleep.

"To hunt up the Mafia," I told the deputy.

I went by the high school and learned that Larry Joe had called in sick the night before, around eight-thirty. He'd said it was a stomach virus and he would be out the rest of the week. The stomach virus reaches epidemic proportions around deer season, an annual medical mystery that employers and principals tactfully overlook.

Inside Larry Joe's house I could hear the wails of three or four small children, a dog barking, and a woman's voice screeching for mercy. I figured the latter must have been from the television, because Joyce was composed when she opened the door. She was a small solemn woman whose hips had gotten away from her after several babies. There were gray

142

streaks in her ponytail and too many lines around her eyes for a woman five years younger than me. The Marauders sweatshirt was faded, the letters almost washed out over the years. She kept the screen door between us, but I didn't much care about being invited in — babies make me nervous.

"Hey, Arly, how are you?"

"I hear Larry Joe's got the flu."

She picked up a baby that had crawled between her feet and settled it on one hip. "That's what he says."

"If he's here, I'm going to have to talk to him, Joyce. You heard about what happened last night?"

"I heard, and it's just awful. Poor Jaylee . . . " She brushed away a snotty-nosed toddler clinging to her leg, then shifted the baby to the other hip and said, "Larry Joe's not here. He and some of his buddies decided to go up to the camp to scout for a stand. They left about ten o'clock last night and won't be back for a couple of days."

"Where's the camp?"

"I don't know, Arly. Larry Joe doesn't tell me that sort of thing. He's always too busy telling me how dirty the house is and how loud and wild the children are." She looked over her shoulder for a moment. "He's right, but there ain't a way to do any better with four children and a teacher's paycheck, moonlighting and all. He won't let me get a real job."

I nodded and left before I started thinking too much about Joyce's life. There wasn't any point in it. I drove over to Jim Bob's house and knocked on the door, wondering what conversations Jim Bob had with his wife.

Mrs. Jim Bob was still in her bathrobe, but her hair was combed and her face painted for the day. She invited me in and suggested coffee. When we were all cozy at the kitchen table, with coffee and a freshly baked cinnamon cake, she told me about the Missionary Society's newest project to raise money for Ethiopian Baptists. Brother Verber was delighted with their efforts, she added with a Cheshire cat sort of smile.

"I have to find Jim Bob," I said gently.

"Why? He doesn't have anything to do with — with what happened to that poor Withers girl. He barely knew her, and he wasn't even in Maggody last night." Mrs. Jim Bob cut me a generous square of cake and slid it across the table on a plate of bone china that matched the cup and saucer to the last rosebud. The lady of the manor, ever gracious to the hired help.

Pride yielded to instinct. "Yummy," I said through a mouthful of crumbs. "If Jim Bob wasn't in town last night, where was he?"

"My husband and his friends went up to their deer camp to tidy up and prepare for the season. I'd presumed they could wait until Friday, but they had me pack some of my fried chicken and potato salad with poppy seed dressing for them, and the last of a baked bean casserole we'd had for dinner. I offered to bake a ham, but they were in too much of a hurry to wait." She pushed the cake around her plate with her fork, then looked up with a bright, girl-to-girl smile. The lady did have a repertoire. "I always say that men can be like little boys when it comes to hunting. Don't you agree?"

"Oh, absolutely. What time exactly did they leave?"

She gave me a superficially puzzled look, but her eyes forgot to participate. "I really couldn't say, Arly, and I'm getting a bit uncomfortable with all these questions about my husband. Are you implying that his absence has something to do with last night's dreadful tragedy?"

I told her that her husband, with a little help from his friends, had kidnapped a bureaucrat and kept him locked up at the motel for four days, although hardly in solitary confinement, then disappeared along with the victim. She sniffed and said she didn't believe a word of it, not a single word, because Jim Bob wasn't like that. I ate some more cake and asked where I might find the deer camp. She gazed out the kitchen window and said she didn't keep up with that sort of thing. I finished the cake and coffee, leaned back in the chair, and asked if she knew what Jim Bob and Jaylee had been discussing in private at the party. She burst into tears. Oops. And I'd been doing so well.

I brought her a box of scented pastel tissues and patted her shoulder while she cried, which I was getting pretty good at, what with all the practice. Once she'd eased up to a steady dribble, I snitched another piece of cake and refilled our cups. When she calmed down, she managed to say she didn't even know Jim Bob had been in the hall next to the kitchen with Jaylee for ten minutes, which was an odd remark, considering I hadn't told her the details.

"Are you sure you don't know where the deer camp is?" I asked once more, praying she was too upset to hear the edge in my voice. "I've got to tell Jim Bob and the others what happened last night, since they can't have heard yet. It's likely that the EPA man is with them, and he's the one who can tell us what happened at the motel last night. I need to question him and turn him over to the state police."

She shook her head, too teary and morose for words, so I thanked her for the coffee and cake and left. Feeling like I had strewn a lot of carnage in my wake, I moved on to the Kwik-Screw for a chat with Dahlia O'Neill and Kevin Buchanon, the wunderkinder of the fast gas business.

"Yeah, I saw Jim Bob last night," Dahlia said, her chin spreading as she nodded. "He was here, then he left."

"What time was he here?" I asked.

"I don't rightly remember. What time do you think it was, Kevin?" She spoke so slowly I felt as if we were in an aquarium, forced to wait while the waves carried the sounds. Kevin shrugged and studied his shoes for oil splashes, leaving Dahlia on the spot. A big fat spot. After a muted belch, she thumped her chest and said, "Well, mebbe it was near ten."

"What did he say?"

"He said to stay out of the storeroom and out of the candy bars," she answered, snickering at Kevin.

"What else did he say?" I said it with forbearance, but my supply was getting depleted as fast as Kevin was turning red.

"He said he wouldn't be back until tomorrow or the next day, because they were going to their deer camp. He took a couple of cases of beer, two bags of ice, and some bologna with him."

"On his shoulders?"

"No, the beer was real heavy. He put the boxes in Roy's pickup."

"Did he take any money out of the cash register?"

"Not that I chanced to see."

Conversation with reticent molasses tries my patience, if not my soul. I steadied myself with a deep breath. "Then Roy was here, too? I am tired of asking questions, Dahlia. I want the whole story – and I want it now!"

"Sure, Arly," Dahlia said goodnaturedly. "Jim Bob met the others – meaning Roy, Larry Joe, and Ho – here about ten. They filled up both vehicles at the self-service, loaded up with food and beer, and left about fifteen minutes later."

"Do you have any idea where the deer camp is?"

"Sorry, Arly." She looked at Kevin, who scuffled his foot on the linoleum floor and shrugged. "Kevin doesn't know either," she added by way of explanation, in case I'd missed the eloquent denial.

"Was there anyone else with those four?"

"Yeah." She reached for a candy bar, but I caught her wrist and gave her a cold stare.

After a pained look at the forbidden wares, she pulled back her hand and said, "There was a man in the back of Jim Bob's jeep. I couldn't tell who it was on account of the blindfold."

Robert Drake opened his eyes to the dusty light filtering through the filthy slit of a window. It took a minute to remember where he was, and why. And how much money he'd lost over the night, although those shitheels would get a surprise when they tried to cash his checks. Everybody always did.

He listened to the erratic drone of snores and snuffles from the front room. It sounded like a kennel, he thought as he rolled over to escape a spring that had gouged him for the better part of three hours. A kennel of goddamn asthmatic bloodhounds. Outside a bird screeched in anger, then flapped away. A fly circled the lightbulb dangling from the ceiling, buzzing as it considered the victim on the bed below. *Snort, snort, snuffle. Caw. Buzz. Snort, snort.* Not a kennel – a goddamn symphony orchestra like the one Dawn Alice was all the time dragging him to so they could look society.

Robert put on his shoes, grabbed his coat, and went into the front room, where he stopped to stare disgustedly at the four men asleep on army surplus cots that looked like rejects from the Civil War or the Revolution. The table was covered with the leftovers of the poker game: beer cans, an empty bourbon bottle, ashes, chips, limp rings of red plastic from bologna, smears of mustard, and bread crusts. And a gold key ring with two keys.

Larry Joe opened one eye. "Where are you going?" he mumbled.

Sliding the glittering key ring into one hand, Robert pointed at the door. "A telegram from my bladder," he said with a sheepish grin. "Be back in a few minutes — unless you want to watch me piss under the table or get dressed so you can come along to guard me."

"Go ahead," Larry Joe said, pulling a drab green blanket over his head. "Don't go too far, you hear? Bears'll get you."

"Right." He eased open the door and stepped outside. There were two vehicles parked on the poor excuse for a road. The keys didn't fit the ignitions of either of them. Snarling under his breath, he went around to the far side of the pickup and pissed on the door for the sheer malice of it.

It was the middle of nowhere; he was surprised there weren't dragons and sea monsters in the thorny underbrush and scrubby-looking trees. The sky was gray, as ugly and scratchy as the blanket under which Larry Joe snoozed blissfully.

The door of the trailer opened. Robert ducked behind the jeep, his shoes sucking mud in the puddle he'd made earlier, and watched Roy take a whiz from the doorway. The door closed. Before he could think, Robert found himself hurrying down the road in a slow lope, his fists brushing the rocks as he made for the shelter of a twisted fir tree. He felt sort of like the wolfman in the middle of transition, but he wasn't about to be spotted from the trailer — not now.

He stopped to catch his breath for a minute while he listened for the sounds of an alarm being raised when his absence was discovered. Nothing happened. He realized that they were unconcerned because they knew they could find him on the road. They'd probably let him walk a long way, to the very limit of the leash, before getting in one of the vehicles to fetch him. The keys had been left on the table as some sort of perverted joke, he figured, flinging them into the woods with a snort of anger.

He straightened up, buttoned his coat, and pushed through the bushes. Downhill, he figured, would get him somewhere. It had to go somewhere; he'd learned that much from movies.

I went back to the PD, grateful that the crowd had thinned out while I was gone. Someone had fetched the table and chairs; Sergeant Plover was seated in the back room next to the coffeepot, while Paulie minded my desk for me. I checked for messages, then coerced my lips into a smile and went to report to Plover.

His table was littered with county survey maps and Styrofoam cups. An ashtray was piled high with butts and gum wrappers, and the whole room stank of male sweat and stale air, neither of which I was particularly fond of. I opened the back door, then turned around to let him enjoy my smile while it lasted.

"Chief," he murmured, pretending he didn't know my name (old Stealthy Plover), "I hope you'll find this arrangement adequate until we wrap up the investigation. I'll try to stay out of your way."

"I hope so. By the way, the missing councilmen are at their deep camp in the woods somewhere. The EPA man is most likely with them, although I don't know that for sure. He was blindfolded and in Jim Bob's four-wheeler just before they left town, so it's a logical assumption they didn't drop him off at the picture show in Starley City. They took enough food for a week. Nobody mentioned weapons, but there's probably an arsenal up there in a closet." I folded my arms and waited for a gasp.

"Where's the deer camp?" he demanded, gasplessly.

"I don't know, and no one would tell me."

He squished his lips together and closed his eyes. "We found the weapon. It had been tossed over the fence behind the motel. It's a cast-aluminum crossbow, brass slides, automatic safety catch, one-seventy-five draw weight, about twelve pounds, and with an accuracy of thirty to thirty-five feet. No prints we could pick up. I sent it on to the lab to confirm that it was used. The shaft was embedded in the back wall of the bathroom; it has an expandable broadhead, which accounts for the size of the wound. You know anyone who might own one?"

"Three-quarters of the male population of Maggody, Sergeant, including the town council, Kevin Buchanon, and my deputy. The crossbow season runs longer, so they can spend more time off work, drinking beer and playing poker with their buddies."

"I don't hunt, myself," he said, sounding apologetic.

"Neither do I," I said.

"Every time I imagine a deer's gentle brown

eyes, I realize I couldn't kill it. I like to watch squirrels and coons, and I can't stand the idea of ripping feathers off a dead bird. I'm the only trooper at the regional headquarters who doesn't bitch about not getting to hunt every day of the gun season."

I looked at him, unable to figure out what his little speech really meant. His gentle brown eyes didn't blink, and I would have had a hard time putting a bullet between them. Honestly. I finally cleared my throat and said, "Have we heard anything from the crime lab in Little Rock?"

"Some preliminary stuff, but they haven't gotten to the autopsy yet. They're guessing she was killed between ten and midnight, although they lean toward the early end of the range, based on body temperature. That would have given her time to make her exit from the party, go home to pack, and start out of town. That's also about the time the councilmen and Drake disappeared. We need to find them in order to ask some pointed questions before we book them for kidnapping."

The four Mafiosi, a beautician, and my mother — what a swell gang of criminals. "Could be somebody in town knows where this deer camp is. Officer Buchanon and I can ask around, see if anybody will talk."

"Is it some kind of secret?"

I was getting too much of the gentle brown for comfort, or maybe the air was too thick with smoke. I squeezed around the table and went to the doorway that led to the front room. "Men are real funny about their territory. They figure there's only so many deer in the area, and they don't want strangers getting there first. Sort of like little boys, don't you think?"

Without waiting for an answer, I told Paulie to see what he could learn about the location of the deer camp. He gave me a half-grin and vacated my desk for the streets of Maggody. I touched up my lipstick, ran a comb through my hair, and followed Paulie out, hoping Plover wouldn't think I was chicken to stay at the PD – with him. Cluck, cluck.

Paulie went south, so I went north to Ruby Bee's. There was not a single pickup parked out front, and the building was locked tight, shades drawn, lights off. The motel sign was off, too. I went around back to Number One, where Ruby Bee lived. She and Estelle were sitting on the couch, tissues clutched in their fists, noses red from being wiped nonstop for several hours.

"Have you been to Jaylee's mobile home?" Ruby Bee whispered.

"Why?" I said it nice and loud.

Estelle gave me a shocked look, as if I'd just hooted "Bingo!" in a funeral parlor. "We've been thinking," she explained softly, so I could appreciate the somberness of the situation and behave with proper decorum.

"I'm impressed. Imagine sitting and thinking at the same time."

"We've been thinking about Jaylee," Estelle continued in the same sepulchral voice, "and her source of income. Ruby Bee paid her handsomely, but a barmaid can only make so much, even including tips. Jaylee wasn't the tiniest bit concerned about the tuition for the Purley Institute, but I am personally aware of the fact it cost seven hundred dollars to earn a certificate. She couldn't work more than part time while she was studying, so she must have been putting some money aside."

"Good point," I admitted, sighing. "I'll call Higgerson at the bank branch and find out if she had a savings account."

Ruby Bee sniffled into her tissue. "Mr. Higgerson said she had less than fifty dollars in savings, and her checking account usually hovered around two hundred dollars. She cleared both of them out yesterday afternoon; the total came to two hundred eleven dollars and eighty-seven cents."

"Mr. Higgerson told you all that? He'd insist

I get a warrant, and I'd still have to drag every bit of it out of him." I gave her a bewildered frown, a shade petulant for good measure.

"Buell Higgerson is a client of mine," Estelle explained grandly. "He thinks the patches of gray make him look more dignified, and he's hoping to become the branch manager soon. He was real pleased to answer my questions when I called to remind him of his next appointment."

"It is a puzzle," Ruby Bee murmured. "Yesterday evening I delicately asked Jaylee if I could loan her a small sum until she got settled, but she laughed and said she would be just fine, that she'd have plenty of money by the time she left town. Estelle and I have been pondering that all morning."

"The state police will be eternally grateful, I'm sure."

"Are you still mad, Ariel?" Ruby Bee grabbed a tissue, prepared for a drawn-out siege.

"Me mad? How utterly absurd! Simply because you made a total fool of me and made me the laughingstock of the county? Now, why would I mind that?" I chuckled at the very idea.

Ruby Bee opted for the offense. "You seem to have forgotten that we did what we did so's we could save Boone Creek from all sorts of pollution and toilet water. We were being ecology-minded, concerned about the environment just like those Green Speech people or the Sierra Madre club. If you'd shown a little more interest in saving the creek, we wouldn't have had to hide Mr. Drake in Number Three."

"I can't argue with that," I said truthfully. "Tell me about Mr. Drake."

Estelle leaned over to touch my knee, a pinched look on her face. "He wasn't nice." She breathed for a few seconds, then added, "He drank too much and used unacceptable language right smack in front of ladies. I went in one time with some paperbacks and a bowl of my cherry cobbler, and he didn't even bother to zip his zipper."

"Dreadful," I breathed right back.

"He was exactly that," Ruby Bee said, equally scandalized by the unsavory memories of the man in Number Three. "He wouldn't eat my biscuits because he said they were made out of ore rock. Now you know perfectly well that my biscuits are as light as a feather, and —"

"Did he have much luggage?" I said before we digressed into swapping recipes or analyzing the volatile baking powder issue.

"He had one suitcase and a briefcase," Estelle said. "He used the briefcase as a portable bar; it had a lemon peel cutter, a tiny jar of olives, a jigger, and a miniature corkscrew. It was right cute and handy."

"It sounds lovely," I said. "Tell me about Jaylee's visits."

Ruby Bee mopped her nose while she studied the chintz under the plastic cover on the couch. I could tell she knew she was on quicksand now, and needed to judge every word so she'd end up righteous instead of hypocritical. The hypocrisy didn't bother her — just my being aware of it.

"I asked Jaylee to take a tray to Mr. Drake Friday night," she finally said. "She didn't come back for a long time, and when she showed up, her hair was mussed and she was pink and puffing like one of them suburban joggers. She admitted that Mr. Drake had gotten fresh with her and that to stop him, she'd been obliged to slap his face. I offered to warn him off, but she said he was real nice under his pretense and she had promised to return to his room later so he could apologize."

"And he apologized several times over the next few days?"

Ruby Bee nodded à la Queen Elizabeth. "That's what she told me, Ariel. She was missing some work, but not enough to cause a problem, so I allowed her to visit whenever she wanted. She was real smitten with him. She said he was educated and had more money than he knew what to do with."

I said that true love was sweet and that I thought I'd better report back to the PD. Everybody seemed to think that was a wonderful idea. The sunshine girls exchanged a few secretive looks (I didn't even wince) and told me to have a nice day. In unison.

Jim Bob slammed the door as he came back into the trailer. "He's gone. I looked around and walked down the road a couple hundred yards, but I didn't see any sign of him."

Ho spun around, his jowls slathered with shaving cream. "Now what, Mr. Mayor? What if he made it to the highway and flagged down a state police car?"

"He didn't make it to the highway. Hell, it's eleven miles as the crow flies and at least sixteen on the road. Our Mr. Drake ain't exactly a boy scout, you know; he's probably sitting on a stump somewhere in the woods wishing he was back here." Jim Bob sat down at the dinette and shoved the trash over the edge. "Listen, boys, today's when Fiff is supposed to get back from his trip, so I'd better go into town and try to get through to him. You all see if you can find Drake and get him back here."

160

Roy and Larry Joe nodded, but Ho wiped his face and said, "I got an automobile dealership to run, Jim Bob. If I'm not there, those assholes I employ as salesmen will hide out in the body-shop lounge, drinking coffee and swapping lies about the bucks they saw and the fish they threw back. Lots of customers want me to sell in person, on account of having seen me on the television commercials. They all want me to do the 'Ho, Ho, Ho's for your best damn deal in the county' bit and get my autograph like I was a celebrity or something. I ain't about to miss sales over your damn fool scheme."

"My damn fool scheme?"

"Come on, Ho," Roy said from his cot, "we're all in this together, like Jim Bob said last night. We've all got things we need to attend to in town, but we have to find Drake first and keep him until Jim Bob talks to Fiff and gets us off the hook. Drake's stupid enough to walk off a bluff or crawl into a cave full of bears. We'd better find him before he gets himself killed and we get blamed for it."

"I'm going into town," Ho said mulishly, thinking again about his terrible trouble that had to stay a secret — at any price — if there was going to be any more *ho, ho, hoing* in Stump County.

Larry Joe came to the dinette and slumped

161

down beside Jim Bob. "What do they do to kidnappers?"

"We didn't kidnap him," Jim Bob said in a pained voice. "We delayed him, and you'd better get that straight. It's not like we killed somebody, for God's sake."

The four men looked at each other, silent.

NINE

Raz Buchanon was in the middle of the front room when I returned to the PD to check in. I decided it would be prudent to leave the door ajar for the next few minutes. Raz was just standing there, his hands in his pockets and his face crinkled up like a bloodhound that had lost the scent.

"I found my bitch," he said.

"Congratulations." I took a quick peek in the back room, but Sergeant Plover was not at the table. I concluded he might have found the need to exit when Raz's aroma drifted through the doorway. He could have left a note. Common courtesy to keep certain people informed about the investigation. I sat down behind my desk and vowed not to breathe. "That's great news about your dog, Raz. You must be feeling easier now that she's back."

"She's dead."

My carefully stored supply of air went out in a whoosh. "Dead? That's terrible! Did – did Perkins shoot her?"

He stuck out his lower lip, which was stained brown from years of chewing tobacco. "Says he didn't. Perkins is a cheater and a liar, so I got no reason to believe him." I hadn't purchased a spittoon or a rusty old coffee can, so the corner once again took the golden arc. "She weren't shot, though, so mebbe Perkins didn't do it." He cackled at his wit.

"Well, that's good to know," I said faintly. "What happened?"

"She was smushed. She must've gotten away from Perkins and tried to cross the highway to get back to my place, being a right loyal bitch and something of a homebody. This morning when I was driving over to the co-op to get some layer scratch, I chanced to see her. She was flatter than a pancake right on the yeller stripe in the middle of the road."

"Are you positive it was–" God, I couldn't remember the name. How humiliating. "– your dog?"

"You implying I wouldn't know Betty, even if she was flat and bloody?" He gave me an indignant look and shot another stream into the corner. "Would you recognize Ruby Bee if'n she got runned over?"

"It was Betty. I believe you, Raz. I'm real sorry about Betty, real sorry. I wish we could have found her and prevented this tragedy. Officer Buchanon did begin the investigation, but we were sidetracked by the kidnapping and then the murder."

"This is murder."

"Raz, she was probably hit by a car passing through town. The driver may not have even noticed when he – he, ah, inadvertently made contact with Betty. Lots of animals get hit on the highway."

"I come to tell you because you are the police and supposed to stop crimes and arrest folks what commit them, not tell the number of skunks and possums that get theirselves run over every night. What are you aiming to do about my bitch?"

I sank back in my chair and rubbed my forehead. Cops on television shows never have to deal with this sort of problem; they have simple, straightforward drug dealers and armed robbers. "When did the crime take place and did anyone happen to see it?" I asked humbly as I pulled out a report form. The ploy had worked before, but I didn't have much hope at the moment. Not with murder on his mind.

"It was last night just before ten. Kevin over at the gas station said he seen the whole thing. It was a big black Mercedes going real fast, mebbe sixty or seventy miles an hour. Didn't even brake for poor Betty or stop afterward to see if he could do something for her. He jest went on through town without any notice of what he did — some damn fool rich man in a hurry."

"You're most likely right, Raz, but I doubt I can do anything since it wasn't a local car. The driver's long gone."

He turned beady eyes on me and sent a splattering finale into the corner. "So's Betty," he said dourly as he went out the door.

I wrote out the silly report, noting the details carefully, and stuffed it in a manila folder in the bottom drawer. I doubted I could convince the State Department of Motor Vehicle Registration to give me a list of black Mercedes, much less track down the owners to see if they had alibis for the night in question. The state boys would hoot for a week, and I had better things to do — just as soon as I figured out what they were.

I was whittling a duck foot when Sergeant Plover returned. Saluting him with my pocket-knife, I kept my attention on the delicate webbing between the toes. A very tricky spot, requiring great care.

"You still trying to turn that hunk of wood into a goose?" he said by way of greeting.

"A marshland mallard," I reminded him coolly. "I picked up a few items of interest while I was investigating, if you want to hear. On the other hand, if you prefer to stand there and make wisecracks about an innocent duck, I'll keep my information to myself."

"Ah, yes, a marshland mallard," he said, nodding like a college professor. "I remember now. There's been admirable progress since I last had the opportunity to admire it." Now he was talking like one, too, so I'd think he was intelligent or at least polite.

"Thank you, Sergeant. I'm pleased with the progress myself. If there's nothing else. . . ?"

"I thought we might exchange information over coffee. I've picked up a few tidbits that might interest you, too."

Once we were settled at his table (in my back room) I told him what I'd learned from Ruby Bee and Estelle via the cosmetology grapevine. We agreed that Jaylee had been pulling a swift one on somebody, and Jim Bob was a prime candidate if we could ever track him down for questioning. Plover then casually dropped the fact that he'd found out the location of the deer camp. It seems he'd stopped by for a comfy little chat with Joyce Lambertino, and she'd finally remembered that Larry Joe's second cousin over in Hasty had been at the camp a few years back. A telephone call later, Plover had the directions in his pocket and an invitation to come back for supper. Slam, bam, thank you, ma'am.

"Nice work," I said.

He gave me a funny glance before pulling out the county map and spreading it out flatter than a runover dog on a yeller stripe. We put our faces over it and finally decided that we knew where the trailer was parked, which was way back in the mountains on some land owned by a Chicago fellow who'd bought it before he discovered there were ticks and snakes along with the deer. He'd made a lease arrangement with the Mafia and confined his hunting to singles' bars.

"I don't think I can find it by myself," Plover admitted. "You'll have to come with me, and we'd probably better get a jeep or four-wheel from the sheriff before we try."

I may have still been a bit miffed over Joyce's flash of brilliance. Of course I hadn't sweet-talked her or gotten myself invited to come back for supper, like I was some encyclopedia salesman with a silver tongue and soft brown eyes.

168

"I intended to go, anyway," I said with a snooty smile as I banged down my coffee cup and walked out. What an exit line.

I called the dispatcher and arranged for a vehicle, then called Paulie and told him where I was going. He said he'd come mind the store. He sounded glum, but I figured it would be his mood for a long time to come, since he'd had a run of personal blows, all about gut height.

Sergeant Plover and I drove to the sheriff's office in his shiny police car. I passed the time admiring all the gizmos on the dashboard and the real live radio that buzzed and snapped like a teenager with bubblegum. My radio comes and goes with no discernible rhythm. Paulie's mostly goes; we've begged the council for new radios at the last dozen meetings, but all we've gotten are lame excuses and harrumphs over the budget. I thought it might be fun to have all the real cop toys – in working condition.

"Can I ask you something, Sergeant Plover?" I said, twisting buttons on the radio to see if I could pick up somebody speaking Spanish.

"You can ask, Chief Hanks."

"Do you have a first name? You don't have to tell me what it is or anything like that – just tell me if you have one."

"I have one."

We looked at each other. "Sergeant," we said

together, like a couple of marionettes on the same set of strings. Damn it, I shouldn't have bothered to ask.

"Ariel isn't going to like this," Ruby Bee whispered, on her knees behind the bush. "She's likely to pitch a fit if she finds out, and I'll never hear the end of it till my ears get so sore they plumb drop off. She's real persistent when she's riled. I used to tell everybody she had her mother's beauty and her daddy's temper."

"She isn't going to get riled because she isn't going to find out," Estelle whispered. She pushed aside a branch for a better view of the mobile home. It looked hollow and cold, an empty box left outside too long. "I don't think the police have even come by here," she added indignantly.

The Pot O'Gold was peaceful. Most of the inhabitants had either returned to work after a midday dinner or had crawled onto a sofa for a nap. A baby had howled for most of an hour, but now it was hushed, tucked in a crib with a bottle of milk. The mother was on a sofa with her own bottle. Paulie had driven by earlier, but he hadn't seen them. Ruby Bee and Estelle had sighed in relief and agreed it was sort of like an omen that God actually wanted them to sneak into Jaylee's mobile home to search for clues. God approved of a lot of their ideas in just such a manner. You could tell if you watched for the signs. An open mind and a liberal interpretation helped.

"My knee hurts," Ruby Bee murmured, shifting her weight as best she could, although gravel was gravel, no matter how careful you were. "How much longer do we have to hide?"

"I don't like this any better than you, but we got to be alert. You're the one who's so all-fired worried about Arly finding out what we're going to do in another minute or two. Eula Lemoy is still out behind her unit taking down the wash from the clothesline. You want her to see us acting like cat burglars?"

Wincing, Ruby Bee crawled to a more advantageous position. "Look at Eula's brassieres, Estelle. They're about as dingy as I've ever seen, and her always going on how's she's a pious Christian woman and president of the Veterans Auxilliary. You'd think she could use less bleach on her tongue and more on her brassieres!"

"Hush up," Estelle whispered. "She's about done. We'll give her a minute to get inside and settled down in front of the television for her soaps, then we'll see if we can figure a way to crawl around to the back of Jaylee's unit. You haven't dropped the key, have you?"

Ruby Bee sniffed as she held up the object in question. "I still say those brassieres are dingy," she whispered crossly. "And my knee still hurts and we're going to get ourselves thrown in the pokey for breaking and entering."

"You've been watching too many of those cop shows, honey. They don't throw criminals in the pokey no more; they just lecture them and probate them so they have to stay out of trouble for the next ten years."

"I dearly hope so," Ruby Bee sighed.

Neither of them saw the daisy-yellow café curtain twitch in the kitchen window of the mobile home.

Robert Drake was sitting on a stump, wishing he was back at the deer camp. Or on the edge of the highway, or at a goddamn ranger station with a telephone and a pot of coffee. Anyplace but the middle of the desolate, cold, stinking woods that seemed to have no end. It had thorns, plenty of those, and holes covered with leaves so you could twist your ankle or sprawl on your face in the mud. Slippery leaves that were wet and slimy when you fell in them. It had noises that you couldn't identify, coming from behind or in front or on both sides. He hadn't seen any animals, but he figured they'd seen him.

It was colder than he realized at first. His coat wasn't nearly heavy enough, and his shoes and socks were soaking wet from a creek crossing that hadn't worked out real well. He was hungrier than he'd ever been in his life, including the time he'd holed up with a cheerleader for thirty-six hours in the Paradise Motel. The mirrors on the ceiling had kept him satiated, along with other activities.

There wasn't much point in just sitting, he told himself as he stood up and studied the woods with a morose sigh. All the trees looked pretty much the same. He'd tried downhill earlier; it had brought him to the bottom of the mountain and the beginning of another one. He'd followed the creek until his feet were blue. Maybe, he thought, he'd go uphill and hope he could see something from the mountaintop – like a highway or some ranger tower. Or a McDonald's burger stand.

"Fat fucking chance," he growled, scrambling up the slope.

Jim Bob and Hobert reached town without problem. Roy and Larry Joe had sworn they'd track Drake down and put him back in the bedroom for the time being. They'd all agreed that Fiff was their only shot, if the asshole would get himself back to his office so he could take Jim Bob's call. Nobody wondered aloud what they'd do if Fiff just laughed and hung up or refused to help them out of what was getting right sticky.

In the front of the car lot, Hobert got out of the four-wheeler and said he'd meet Jim Bob in an hour or so, as soon as he kicked some ass and got his sales force in gear. But once Jim Bob had driven away, Ho hurried to his office and locked the door. He squatted down and opened the safe, hoping that somehow there would be enough money, that the lovely green stuff had begat more in his absence.

It hadn't, and there wasn't enough. He slammed the safe closed, sat down at his desk, and glared at the paperwork awaiting him. No way he could get to it now, he thought, his jowls turning pale as he considered what was likely to happen when he admitted he didn't have two thousand dollars in cash. Carl Withers wasn't the sort to slap him on the back and laugh about the delay. No, Carl was more apt to inflict pain — serious pain and permanent damage. Ho shivered at the images racing through his mind. It was a damn bad business. He had to come up with some way to get out of it, without getting himself killed or his reputation torn to shreds.

"How long will it take us to get to the camp?" Plover asked as we drove away from the sheriff's office in a bright red jeep.

"At least an hour. The road's probably washed out, and we have to cross the creek in a couple of places. If nothing else happens, we may find that we're wrong about the location of the deer camp, that it's on one of the other hundred roads back in the hills." I gazed through the windshield at a scrawny cow, who gazed back with Dahlia's serene lack of comprehension. "And they may not be there, in any case. This has the feel of a wild goose chase, Sergeant Plover."

"Or a marshland mallard hunt."

"Something like that, too," I said, smiling just a little bit to prove I had a sense of humor. I pointed out the place to turn, then settled back and studied him out of the corner of my eyes. Not with any warmth, mind you, but out of curiosity. "Do you have any influence with the boys at the state police academy?"

"They don't call me when they need a light-bulb changed, but I guess I know some of the instructors."

I told him about the letter that had shattered Paulie's dream. He pointed out that not more than one in fifty made it to the academy, and even passing the tests would not guarantee a slot in the next class. We both agreed (odd) that Paulie ought to settle for the regular academy or try something in another direction, but I still felt sort of sad. I did not break into "The Impossible Dream" at this point, nor did I hum a few bars of "Climb Every Mountain," even though the idea came to mind.

As expected, the road got a lot worse as we twisted our way through the mountains. It was chilly in the deep valleys, and the wind was severe on the higher cuts. To keep myself from turning blue, I asked my driver what he thought about the investigation.

"There's something I haven't told you yet," he said. "I was going to tell you earlier, but you flounced out of the room before I had a chance."

"I left the room at a briskly professional pace in order to arrange for the jeep," I pointed out through clenched teeth. "You suggested we needed to call the sheriff, Sergeant. I was merely cooperating with you, since you have rank and serial number, if not name."

"Why'd your mother name you Ariel?"

"Ariel's a character in *The Tempest*, a blithe, gossamer spirit who stirs up mischief. 'I come to answer thy best pleasure; be't to fly, to swim, to dive into the fire, to ride on the curled clouds.' "

"Oh," he said, properly awed. "Do you do all that stuff?"

"What stuff?"

"Dive into fire and fly through curled clouds?"

"When the mood strikes me."

After a moment of silence, he said, "What I didn't tell you earlier was that I got the initial report from the coroner at the state lab. It seems Miss Withers was approximately seven weeks pregnant."

"What? Were they sure? After all, Carl's been unavailable for that sort of thing for nearly two years. I presume they don't allow inmates to stick it through the wire mesh on visitation days, and we haven't gotten to the point of conjugal visits at Cummins yet."

"So it wasn't her husband. Surely Miss Withers knew more than one male in Maggody, and thus far I've gathered she wasn't the sort to sit home chastely and bake cookies for her husband."

"Not exactly, no. Jaylee did date; in fact, she had Paulie all hot to trot, but I don't think she let it get that far with him." I toyed with a handful of the puzzle pieces for a few minutes. "But she'd certainly fool around with Jim Bob Buchanon. He could afford an occasional little trinket or a night in Starley City, and he's not

177

too terrible to look at — if you keep your eyes closed in bed. I'll bet that what was I overheard during the party — Jaylee telling Jim Bob the news and demanding some money to keep quiet."

"Do you?"

"Do I what?"

"Keep your eyes closed in bed?"

Despite my mental lecture, I turned pinker than a milk cow's udder. I flapped my mouth a couple of times, but I couldn't get anything out, so I finally gave up and stared at the woods as if I'd never seen them before. I could hear him chuckling, but I wasn't about to acknowledge it.

"Do you think Jim Bob would kill Jaylee to keep her from blackmailing him?" he asked. "Is he that type?"

"He's not a paragon of virtue, but I don't know if he'd go that far just to keep her quiet. Mrs. Jim Bob wouldn't take kindly to the news he'd fathered a bastard with the local barmaid, and she'd be likely to throw him out on his ear while she sulked, but she'd take him back in once he had suffered enough. I can't see him murdering Jaylee to avoid a spot of discomfort."

"But would he pay her off?"

"Possibly. We ought to be there in another fifteen to twenty minutes. I'll take real pleasure in asking His Honor all about it."

The *Mephitis mephitis* (Mustelidae) was startled out of a dream by the crackle of leaves above its head. Suddenly a shoe landed on its body, hard and frightening, squashing its fur and causing great pain along the tail and the small, delicate hind leg. A muffled expletive followed.

The *Mephitis mephitis* was too alarmed to roll over and go back to a blissful dream of grubs and birds' eggs for breakfast. With a growl, it scurried out of the indentation, turned its hindquarters toward the invader, and lifted its tail. A fine mist of yellow liquid sprayed out. This produced a loud bellow and a series of coughs and sputters, followed by more expletives and a tumbling, terrified retreat. The *Mephitis mephitis* (also called polecat or zorrino, or sometimes wood pussy) gave the invader a beady look, then shuffled away to find another bed until evening. Its black and white tail swished indignantly as it disappeared into a thicket.

"Holy shit," moaned Robert Drake.

"My knees are going to freeze up in another minute," Ruby Bee hissed. "Eula's been inside a good ten minutes, and I'm cold. I didn't come here to hunker in the bushes and —"

"Then stop your bitching and come on," Estelle said. She stood up, then dashed for the back of the mobile home, praying Eula didn't feel the need for a cup of tea during the commercial. Ruby Bee pounded along behind her, and the two reached the back door without hearing any hollers or cries aimed at them.

With trembling hands, Ruby Bee unlocked the door and slipped in like a tubby bolt of greased lightning, her partner in crime on her heels. Estelle closed the door, leaned against it, and put her hand on her chest.

"We made it," she panted. "I just knew Eula was going to see us, or Bart Harkins on the other side. I don't know what we could have told them that wouldn't sound right suspicious."

"Now that we're here, what do we aim to do?"

"We went over that before, Ruby Bee. We got to find proof that Jaylee was getting money from somebody in Maggody — like Jim Bob, for instance. You take the bedroom and I'll start in the kitchen."

Ruby Bee looked over her shoulder at the dark hallway and the closed doors. There was a musty odor, as if something had died and been left to rot in a closet, and there was a presence of danger that was thicker than her best pan gravy. A chill raced up her back. "I think we ought to stick together," she whispered.

"We already decided that would take too long," Estelle said impatiently. "You ain't afraid of finding a spook, are you?"

Ruby Bee realized that Estelle had hit the nail square on the head. "Of course not. But if we search together, we can do each room twice as fast. Besides, I might stumble onto something and not be sure if it was important. If you were there, we could decide faster."

"All right, but I think you're behaving like a kid. There ain't no such thing as spooks, Ruby Bee Hanks, and the Lord knows you ought to have learned that much in the last fifty-five years."

"Why, Estelle Oppers, you know perfectly well I'm fifty-three!"

"Then you'd better go back to grade school and practice your subtraction! You are two years older than me, which makes you fifty-five if you're a day old!"

"Am not."

"You are, too! You think I can't keep track of my own birthdays, Missus Hanks? I am fifty-three — which makes you fifty-five! We'll just pull out my birth certificate and see!"

"That doesn't prove nothing!"

Carl Withers, who was crouched behind the refrigerator, felt his temper begin to boil. He'd planned to jump out at them and scare them off, then grab the food he'd put in a grocery sack and hightail it out of there. Now the two old biddies sounded like they were going to rip each other up out in the living room over some fool woman thing.

He didn't have all day to wait around while they gabbed at each other. He eased around the refrigerator and carefully opened a drawer. Taking out a knife, he felt a sudden warmth in his lower body. Shit, it might be fun.

TEN

Somebody must have been watching over us, because we saw the trailer sitting in a clearing about where I'd thought it would be. It was dingy, battered, and squatty, its belly overgrown with vines and weeds, its front door liable to blow off in the next good wind. About standard for such things, I decided, as we pulled to a stop behind a green pickup truck. Deer camps aren't known for their luxurious accommodations or scenic settings. Or plumbing, I added as I saw a half-fallen outhouse behind the trailer. Just by looking at it, I could feel the spiders crawling up my leg.

"That pickup belongs to Roy Stivers," I told Sergeant Plover. "I expected to see Jim Bob's four-wheel around here, too. I wonder where in tarnation he's run off to."

"Somebody's here. I saw a face in the window." He cut off the engine and took out a handkerchief to clean his sunglasses, showing no inclination to storm the trailer. "Let's sit here for a while."

I was a little disappointed with his laid-back approach. "Shouldn't we do something?" I suggested.

"And get ourselves blown to kingdom come by a shotgun? I've got too much respect for my backside to go rushing up to the door with my gun drawn. We'll just sit a spell and see what happens."

"Is that what they teach at state police school?"

He gave me a slow, shit-eating grin. "Yep."

"And how to sell tickets to the state troopers' ball?"

"State troopers don't have balls."

"So I noticed."

After about five minutes of silence, Roy came to the door of the trailer and said, "Whatcha doing, Arly? Don't you want to come and visit for a while? It's pretty damn cold out there, and you are all welcome to some beer and sandwiches if you're hungry."

I ignored Plover's muffled laugh and marched across the weeds. "Who else is in there, Roy?"

"Larry Joe's here right now, and Ho and Jim

Bob'll be back pretty soon. You sure you don't want to come in and sit a spell?"

"Thank you very much," I said, shooting a haughty look over my shoulder in the general direction of the Nameless Wonder, who was still in the jeep where he'd taken root. "My driver seems to prefer to wait outside."

"Oh, I'm coming," Plover said. After he untangled his legs from under the wheel, he ambled over to my side and motioned for me to precede him. The man was such a prince, especially when it came to allowing me to see if there was going to be a twelve gauge aimed at my face when I stepped inside.

Actually, there was only Larry Joe's affable smile and an incredible miasma of stale beer and cigar smoke. "Nice place you got here," I said. "Where'd Jim Bob and Hobert run off to, by the way? We didn't see them on the road."

"You must have just missed them. They went into town a couple hours ago," Roy said. "How about a bologna sandwich, Arly? The bread's a mite stale, but it hasn't turned blue yet."

"Maybe later. When are they getting back?"

Larry Joe's face went pale. "Why are you asking all these questions about Jim Bob and Ho? Is there some special reason you and this fellow here want to talk to them?"

185

"We all came up here to scout a stand before the season," Roy said. "Play poker and brag. It ain't exactly a crime."

Sergeant Plover took a beer out of the cooler and opened it with a swoosh. "Kidnapping is," he said.

"Who got hisself kidnapped?" Larry Joe said. Or squeaked, to be more precise. He went even paler, until he matched the slice of bread on the table in front of him. Good thing it wasn't blue – I almost flunked my CPR course at the academy.

"A contract liaison from the EPA regional office in Dallas," Plover said. "Man's name is Robert Drake, about five foot six, dark hair and eyes, no distinguishing scars."

"What makes you think we might know something about that?" Roy said, his eyes narrowed and his mouth twisted to one side. He even went so far as to put his hands on his denim hips. A nice bluff.

"Because you and the others locked him in Number Three at the Flamingo Motel on Friday." Plover took a drink of beer. "Then you checked him out last night and brought him here. Is he tied up in the back somewhere?"

Larry Joe buried his face in his hands, moaning softly. Roy gulped several times, then turned on me. "This fellow's crazier than Raz's eldest girl. I'd like to think you don't believe his fairy tales, Arly."

I could see my rent rising faster than Boone Creek in May. "Ruby Bee and Estelle already admitted their part in it," I said apologetically. "It came out when the body was found."

"Whose body?" Roy snapped. He didn't look real good, either; it was even money who'd go first — him or Larry Joe.

I told them about Jaylee. When I finished, Larry Joe was nearly sobbing, and Roy was perched on the edge of an army cot, white and darn close to comatose. Plover finished his beer and motioned for me to join him in the filthy kitchenette.

"Keep an eye on these two while I see if I can find Drake. They don't look capable of trying anything, but you never know. You have any bullets in your gun?" I nodded. He went into the bedroom, then came out with a frown. "Nobody there. I'm going to look outside."

"Holler if you need me," I said.

I received another funny look before he went outside. Since I didn't know what it meant, I forgot about it and sat down on the cot next to Roy. "Tell me what happened to -the EPA fellow. Kidnapping's serious, but murder's a damn sight more serious. Jaylee was visiting Drake in his room on a regular schedule. Now

187

she's dead and he's missing. I've got to find him, Roy."

"He ran off early this morning," Roy said in a wooden voice. "Larry Joe and I searched the whole side of the ridge for him, but we couldn't find any trace of him. He probably got hisself eaten by a bear. Did he — did he kill Jaylee?"

"I haven't had a chance to ask him. He was your prisoner, not mine. Where was he last night after nine o'clock?"

"We collected him about eight and put him in Ho's trunk while we split up to get our gear. We met at ten o'clock behind Jim Bob's store, transferred the fellow to the back of the four-wheel, and left right after that. He was here all night. I'm sure of that because we sat up all night playing cards, and he dropped nearly two hundred dollars. He doesn't have the card sense God, gave a duck."

"So he was locked in Ho's trunk when you left the others about eight and went home?"

"That's correct, Arly. Nobody called or came by while I was packing, but I was in the back of the antique store right up to ten o'clock."

I looked at Larry Joe, who was slumped over the table but breathing a little bit better. "What about you, Larry Joe? What'd you do between eight and ten o'clock last night?"

"I went home, told Joyce what we were

doing, and called in sick to the principal's house. Then I kissed the kids goodbye, grabbed up my sleeping bag and some clothes, and went to the Kwik-Screw to meet everybody." He hiccuped gently. "Joyce will back my story if'n she has to, and I didn't have any reason to hurt Jaylee."

I sat and thought for a long time. It didn't sound like Drake could have killed Jaylee, even if I could come up with a motive. Which would have been tough, since Jaylee was probably keeping him nicely entertained. Larry Joe and Roy didn't have any motive I could dream up on the spur of the moment. It occurred to me that Jim Bob had at least two motives: blackmail and/or jealousy.

"Why'd Jim Bob and Ho go into town?" I asked.

"Senator Fiff was supposed to get back from Las Vegas and be in his office today. We was hoping Friday when we waylaid Drake that Fiff would do something to halt the EPA from allowing Starley City to dump their shit in Boone Creek. But Fiff wasn't around, so we had to wait until today to telephone him."

"That is the stupidest thing I've heard in a long time," I told Roy disgustedly. "You committed a felony, involving my mother along the way, so you could get Fiff to save the creek?"

Before he could answer, Sergeant Plover came back into the trailer. "He's not anywhere around here. There're some footprints in a circle of mud out front, but no sign of him."

I told him what Roy had told me. We all looked at one another for a long time, then Plover sat down at the dinette across from Larry Joe. "Guess we'd better wait for Jim Bob and Ho to return," he said.

It was as good as anything I could suggest, so I settled for a glare at Roy and a regal nod for the room at large.

Robert Drake had never been so utterly miserable in his life, so wet and cold, so nauseated from his own stinking body, so weak from trying not to breathe until his lungs threatened to explode. His half-blinded eyes teared continually, sending dribbles down his neck and under his shirt, where they seemed to turn to ice. His feet stumbled forward, each step a lurching spasm that put him on his hands and knees more often than not. His palms were bloodied, his legs so numb he wasn't sure they were there.

He'd quit cursing the skunk an hour ago, mostly because he was too tired and sick to think of any more four-letter words. Several times after falls he'd lingered for a few minutes

190

in the wet leaves, considering just staying down until he froze to death. But the stink would push him to his feet, as if he might escape himself if he moved ahead quickly enough. He just didn't know where.

At least he wasn't bothered by the noises of animals in the underbrush around him or birds scolding him from the trees. They had deserted him after the incident, their noses and beaks pinched closed in disgust. Did anything ever smell quite so bad? Could a person die from the fumes that hovered around him like a foul green cloud?

He kept thinking about Dawn Alice, the conniving bitch who caused all his trouble. Starting up tennis lessons at her age, as if she had the body to romp all over the court without a bra, letting her boobs flop like rubber chickens for the benefit of the tennis pro! He'd put a stop to that once and for all when he got home. She could sit home and stare at the wall, but she sure as hell wasn't going to whang the tennis pro's balls anymore. He'd see to that, and wring her neck if she even tried to leave the house. If the pro showed up, he'd kill him, too. Kill them both. Leave their bodies draped over the net. He repeated his plan over and over in a singsong whisper.

As he pushed through a clump of firs, he saw

Dawn Alice at the edge of the tennis court, the clubhouse behind her. No bra, of course, and a sheen of perspiration on her forehead from humping in the pro shop. She had a racket in one hand. He ignored her startled look and lunged at her, screaming, "Goddamn you, you bloody bitch! I told you that you weren't going to play tennis anymore! I'm going to rip your smirk off your goddamn face!"

He never saw the shovel that smacked the back of his head, but he heard Dawn Alice laughing as he crumpled down in the mud in front of the clubhouse.

"If I wanted to, I could mail-order a birth certificate and write in whatever date I wanted to," Ruby Bee said, grinding her teeth as she glared up at Estelle. "I could make like I was eighteen years old if I wanted to. But that wouldn't make it gospel, would it?"

"You have totally lost your mind. I ought to call the insane asylum and have them put you away, Ruby Bee Hanks – before everybody finds out how crazy you are."

"Well, I never! Let me tell you another thing, Miss Oppers."

They were never going to quit, Carl decided wearily. The knife handle was damp in his palm, the blade tapping against his thigh in an impatient, silent rhythm. He'd hovered just inside the doorway for a long time, all set to grab one of them around the neck while he stuck the knife in the other one's throat and ordered them to shut their damn traps if they didn't want to see a lot of blood. They'd even moved toward the kitchen at one point, and he'd gotten on his toes, licking his lips and swaying eagerly. Then they'd retreated to the middle of the room. Women. They kept telling each other who was crazier, but Carl figured he was getting crazier than the both of them put together.

If they didn't get back to business pretty damn quick, he was going to have to go after them. His leg was useless now, so swollen he couldn't feel anything but pain and fire. Chasing them around the living room was going to put him in a bad mood once he caught them. Just like when he was a kid and had been sent to catch a chicken for Sunday dinner — he'd taken real pleasure in twisting the scrawny neck so slowly it took a long time for the final death squawk. The broads in the other room had scrawny necks, too. He wondered how they'd feel in his fingers.

Jim Bob stomped into the Kwik-Screw, told Dahlia to lay off the candy bars once and for all or he'd slap her up against the wall, and went into his office. He called Fiff's office and sat down behind his genuine oak veneer desk, praying the twit hadn't decided to stay an extra week in Las Vegas. After a few choice cuss words for the receptionist on the other end of the line, he found himself speaking to the Honorable Fiff himself.

He decided to ease into the situation. "Those damn fools in Dallas okayed Starley City's construction grant, Fiff. They sent some sort of liaison to check out the contract. What are you going to do about it — we don't want shit in the creek."

"Why, Jim Bob, it's good to hear your voice again. How's Mrs. Jim Bob?"

"She's fine," he said, not knowing or caring. "You've got to throw a monkey wrench in this EPA nonsense. You're the elected representative and you're supposed to care about your constituency if you plan to get elected again next year."

"Of course I do, Jim Bob; I take great pride in serving the people of my district, even if it means late nights with the candle burning away at both ends. Hold on for a minute while I have my secretary round up the paperwork on this here sewage disposal plant. I been out of state for several days, doing an analysis of one of my

194

colleague's pork-barrel projects. I have to watch every penny of the taxpayers' dollars." He chuckled, then covered the receiver and gave out some orders too muffled for Jim Bob to get. "You and the boys all het up for the deer season?" he added.

"Just get the papers, Fiff," Jim Bob snarled.

The line rustled, and he could hear Fiff humming under his breath as he shifted papers. After a long minute, Fiff cleared his throat and said, "On the face of it, this appears to be in order, Jim Bob, and there ain't a thing I can do about it. Lemme see . . . Yep, the BOD and TSS are right at ten parts per million, as specified in our great country's Federal Water Quality Act, and the phosphorous and ammonia are going to be right good. I remember you telling me about this before, Jim Bob, but I don't think you have any cause to worry about it anymore. Your creek'll be plumb full of bass and crappies, and I'll come over to catch a string and prove it to you."

"That's the shit they've been giving us at those damn fool 'public participation forums' — and what it means is shit! Can't you file a protest with the federal boys so this can be delayed until we've filed another petition for relief? The final papers haven't been signed as of yet."

"I could, Jim Bob, but you got to remember that Starley City has twenty-two thousand fine and upstanding constituents, while Maggody's got a scant handful. Politics is tricky, and I don't want to offend anybody if I can help it, but the naked truth is that I've got to bend to the biggest breeze."

"You windbag," Jim Bob said, his face purple as he clutched the receiver in a death grip. "You told me one night at the poker table that you'd do something about this, and —"

"Let's get together and play another time," Fiff said genially, overriding the continued sputters and threats with practiced ease. "I had myself a real nice time that night, even if you boys romped me like I was a virgin in the locker room. Thanks for calling, and get yourself a twelve-point buck next week. Take care and have a good day."

Jim Bob dropped the receiver and sank into the chair. When the door opened five minutes later, he hadn't moved further than a rat's hair, and his face was rigid.

"Hey, Jim Bob," Dahlia said, wondering why he looked like something the cat threw up, "did you hear about Jaylee?"

"Jaylee's gone to Little Rock. I know that much."

"No she ain't. She got herself murdered last

night, over behind Ruby Bee's Bar and Grill. Kevin said he heard she was naked in one of the motel rooms, with an arrow smack dab in her tit."

"What brand of shit are you trying to feed me?" Jim Bob said, turning purpler. "Your brain's too stuffed with chocolate to know what your mouth is babbling. Get out of here and get your ass back to work before I transport it with my boot!"

"Dahlia is essentially right," Mrs. Jim Bob said, gliding past the barricade in the doorway to sit on the couch. She placed her purse on the floor, crossed her ankles, and folded her hands in her lap. "Jaylee was found last night, murdered. Kevin has perhaps exaggerated the melodrama of the scene, but Jaylee Withers is really and truly dead. Murdered. Arly was up at the house to ask you some questions this morning, and she sounded like her questions were going to be more pointed than a piece of barbed wire. I told her that you were out. I did not offer the details of your tawdry affair, but I may change my mind and give her a call after we chat."

Dahlia's mouth fell open and her cheeks ballooned out as she turned to stare at Mrs. Jim Bob. She wished Kevin was there to hear it, too. It sounded like it was going to be real interesting.

Jim Bob wondered if somebody upstairs was a mite peeved with him.

Paulie decided to see if he could find any clues at Jaylee's mobile home. Not like a state trooper would, of course — just like a hick small-town deputy who wasn't even a graduate of the police academy. In four months he'd have to quit the Maggody force, since he probably couldn't even get in the academy if he tried — couldn't get in anywhere. He wondered if he would end up as a night watchman at the Pot O'Gold, or pumping gas and diddling Dahlia at the Kwik-Screw while she ate a gross of candy bars and offered helpful hints on technique.

He and Jaylee had been close. Hell, they'd been right on the edge of escaping Maggody, of making something of themselves and seeing how real folks lived. Jaylee had been closer than he, of course, since she'd passed her GED and been accepted at the cosmetology institute. He'd flunked two out of three parts of the test.

"I still could've gone with her," he said under his breath as he climbed into the police car and drove to the Pot O'Gold. Jaylee's mobile home was parked near the back fence, which she'd liked. She always said she could watch the pasture for hours on end, although Paulie had never thought it was all that exciting a view. Bunch of dumb cows.

He slowed down for the cattle guard at the gate, then drove very slowly down the road, one eye on the kids playing in a drainage ditch. Kids were stupid enough to dart right into the road without a single look to see if a car was coming. Carl Withers had tried to prove the Buchanon boy had done just that the night of the hit-and-run, but he'd also admitted he was drunk and driving a stolen vehicle, so the judge didn't pay much heed to any of Carl's defense. Jaylee talked about it for a long time, as if he'd been the least bit interested in Carl Withers's crimes.

Paulie slammed on the brakes as a ball bounced off the hood of his car. He saw the culprits as they dodged under a clothesline, scrambling like a flock of dirty-faced monkeys. He considered whether he ought to go after them, if only to put the fear of God in them. Maybe a lecture, all stern and official, making sure they saw the regulation gun at his side. Kids always got wide-eyed when they saw the gun. If they apologized for the negligence with the ball, he might even let them touch the holster.

But he'd never get them now; they'd hightailed it to one of their holes, where they'd hunker down and tell each other, What a close call that was! Did you see the way he stared at us?

He reluctantly decided to allow them to escape without punishment this time. He continued at a snail's pace down the road to Jaylee's unit, cut off the engine, and picked up a notebook and his fingerprint kit. The chief didn't know he had one; he'd ordered it from some company in Michigan that advertised in the back of men's magazines. He doubted he would find any prints that he could identify, since the only ones he had in his notebook were his own and his mother's, but he could at least try a few surfaces. He might find something worth sticking in his notebook.

He opened the car door, but he couldn't bring himself to get out and start playing detective. Poor Jaylee, he thought, remembering how she used to try crazy hairstyles, then call him to come over and judge them for originality or some dumb thing like that. He'd always admired her efforts, even if it made her look like somebody had run her through the rinse cycle of a washing machine. One night when he'd come by, she had a big orange stripe down the middle of her head and green patches over her ears. She'd informed him it was punk, and he'd had to grit his teeth not to laugh. Jaylee'd been real serious about her career in cosmetology. It was hard to overlook some of her other interests, though. Hell, it was downright impossible not to dwell on what he knew she'd been doing with other men. A spark of pain hit his gut, and he pushed the thought aside before it could eat at his insides like some vile, red-eyed rat. He suspected the rat was going to be there for a long time to come.

Her mobile home (she never allowed anyone to say "trailer") seemed sad without her laughter drifting through the door. He made himself walk up the little path she'd lined with gay plastic daisies and embedded with white bricks, then halted by the door to compose himself. Which was when he heard the conversation coming from inside the mobile home.

Paulie whipped out his gun and fumbled for a bullet. Hell, two. One for each of the prowlers in there desecrating Jaylee's home and stealing every damn thing they could find. He cautiously tested the front-door knob, a bead of sweat popping out at each tiny squeak. Locked. He moved to a window and tried to peek through the blinds, but they were tightly drawn. The murmurs sounded urgent, as if something was about to happen while he hung around outside, clutching his gun and unable to defend Jaylee's home. He wasn't sure there was time to try the back door.

"Paulie Buchanon! What are you doing with your gun? Don't you go and shoot your foot again!" Eula stood in the doorway of her mobile home, a cup and saucer in one hand and a *TV Guide* in the other.

He gestured for her to shut up. "Call the sheriff's office and tell them to send a backup unit," he whispered.

"For Ruby Bee and Estelle? Oh, Paulie Buchanon, you are a scream! Can you imagine their faces if some big sheriff's deputy came pounding on the door?"

"Ruby Bee and Estelle are in there?" He lowered the gun, reluctantly. "You sure about that, Eula?"

"I seen them with my own eyes when they snuck around to the back door and went inside. I told Mr. Harkins they looked like they were playing cops and robbers, silly old women! He said he'd never heard such nonsense in his life."

Sighing, Paulie removed the bullets and put them in his pocket, replaced the gun in its holster, then pounded on the door with his fist. "You open up in there, Ruby Bee! Estelle, I know you're in there, too, so you just open this door before I get any madder than I already am!"

The door opened. Ruby Bee waved him in, looking real downcast about getting caught. Which she damn well ought to be, Paulie told himself. Estelle was sitting on one end of the sofa, and she didn't look very happy either. As he opened his mouth for the introductory words of what was going to be a long lecture, Ruby Bee pointed to a figure behind the door.

"You remember Carl Withers, don't you? Carl, this is Paulie Buchanon. His parents own the Pot O'Gold, and Paulie's a deputy on the local police force."

Introductions over, conversation came to a standstill. Carl showed Paulie the knife in his hand and gestured for him to sit by Estelle. Ruby Bee joined them. Carl came over and pointed at Paulie's gun. It passed hands, along with both of the bullets. Carl peeked through the curtains, his brow scrunched up real tight. The three on the couch squeezed together, although they did not arrange their hands over their eyes, ears, and mouths respectively.

"Snoopy bitch," Carl breathed. He looked over his shoulder. "You really screwed up, you broads. If you'd stayed clear of the mobile home, I would have been able to get the payoff and get my ass out of this crappy town. Now I'm stuck with you — and this Deputy Dawg character. One of you fix me something to eat, and the other see if there's medicine and bandages in the bathroom, anything to ease the pain in my leg."

"Oh, my goodness," Ruby Bee said, staring at his leg. "That looks awful. It must be hurting you real bad by now, and I think you'd better go straight to the hospital and get it attended to by a doctor."

Carl gave her a smile, albeit not too warm. "If I did that, they'd want me to scoot back to prison, wouldn't they?" He waited until the three on the couch nodded, then said, "It's hard to understand if you haven't been there, but prison is not my idea of a real good time. For one thing, they lock you up all the time. They also are insistent that you hoe fields in the hundred-degree heat, eat slop pigs wouldn't touch, and spend time with bad men. You wouldn't want me to go back, would you?" He waited until they shook their heads. "Now how about some food and medicine, if you could get your asses up and in action before I cut somebody's throat!"

He pulled back the curtain again and scowled at the scattered mobile homes and road. Once he'd concluded his business, he realized he'd have to do something with his three idiotic prisoners. If he left them behind, he wouldn't reach the county line without a battalion of police cars wailing down the highway after him.

"Get that attended by a doctor," he said in a squeaky, bitter falsetto. "Get yourself carved up, lady."

E L E V E N

It was getting pretty boring in the deer camp trailer. Larry Joe was enthralled by the tips of his shoes, and Roy was meandering through his own thoughts, which probably weren't altogether cheerful from the way he studied the wall. Sergeant Plover appeared to be in the middle of a nap. I wasted most of an hour considering the wisdom of a permanent versus a haircut and finally decided to do nothing rash for another year or two.

The current theory was that Jim Bob and Ho would be back in another hour, if they hadn't been detained in town or stopped by a flat tire on the road. Plover had communicated with the sheriff's office, and they had agreed to keep an avuncular eye on the two but not stop them. They'd promised to search the back side of the ridge for the kidnappee, but they'd also muttered something about the size of said woods, haystacks, and pine needles. In the meantime, we were hoping Drake would stumble out of the underbrush to explain himself. Mostly we were sitting.

"Anybody want to play cards?" I said. I got blank looks from three different directions, but at least Plover wasn't asleep on the job. "We don't have to, guys. It was a suggestion, that's all. We've been sitting here a long time and I'm bored, but maybe I'll take a walk instead."

I stood up, but Plover caught my arm and pulled me back down. "That's a good idea, cards. You know how to play poker?"

"I was thinking of canasta."

Roy and Larry Joe started shaking their heads, and even Plover looked nonplussed. Don't men ever play anything but poker? "Oh, all right," I said. "I'll play poker, if someone will write down what beats what. I always get confused with straights and flushes, but I happen to be a very good poker player. We used to play all the time at the dorm at college, after we got in from our dates. Who deals first?"

Everybody looked a darn sight more cheerful as they scooted chairs around the table and started counting chips. Roy offered to open a round of beers, and Larry Joe said he would make some sandwiches after a few hands.

Plover took out his wallet and extracted a wad of bills. "Let's consider ourselves off duty until we hear something. What's the limit?"

"I say a dollar," Roy said. He looked at me, no doubt thinking he was gazing at dead meat. "Dollar okay with you, Arly?"

"A dollar a hand is fine with me," I replied. I downed half my beer in a gulp and wiped my mouth on my sleeve, trying to get in the proper frame of mind. I even managed a delicate belch.

"A dollar limit on bets," Roy said, pained but gentle. "Three raises, no check and raise, dealer's choice, first jack deals, and if nobody cares, I'll run the bank."

We didn't do all that stuff in the dorm, but it sounded okay with me. I took out a five-dollar bill and tossed it on the table. "I'm ready when you are, gentlemen. By the way, what's wild?"

For some reason, they thought that was a riot. Nobody laughed out loud, but I could see them fighting it. I decided to fleece them for every last penny. No mercy. Not even for the Nameless Wonder, who was trying the hardest not to laugh.

"Deal the cards," I commanded in a cold voice.

Robert Drake opened his eyes slowly, shuddering as his head exploded with pain. His eyes refused to focus at first, but at last he blinked away the hazy blur. There was a ceiling above him, and shafts of light that came through the numerous cracks like knife blades. He realized he was inside a house of some kind, a ramshackle shanty from the looks of the ceiling. For a moment, he thought it stank worse than a pigsty, but then he remembered the source of the stench and closed his eyes.

It had to be a nightmare. Nothing like this could happen to him, a bright, semi-young civil servant with two cars, a ranch house with a swimming pool right off the patio, membership in the right country club, and a wife who — his eyes shot open hard enough to bruise his eyebrows.

He'd seen Dawn Alice. The clubhouse and the tennis court. He'd tried to get her, but something had stopped him in the middle of the lunge. It'd stopped his head, anyway. Had he managed to throttle Dawn Alice while unconscious? God, he hoped so.

It didn't exactly explain where he was, why his head hurt worse than any hangover he'd ever had (and he'd had some doozies), or where he was. Not the woods; he could tell that much. Heaven didn't sound probable, and he wasn't about to dwell on the alternative. It was too damn cold, for one thing; the wind blew through the room as if the walls didn't exist. The ceiling didn't stop much either; there'd be a goddamn monsoon inside when it rained.

He was on a bed of sorts, covered with a scratchy tattered quilt that looked brown until you noticed a few white creases that had missed the dirt. The mattress felt as if it were stuffed with dried corncobs. Nothing remotely resembled sheets or pillows.

He was also buck naked. He thought about that for a long time, but an explanation didn't come. It sure wasn't some kinky hospital where they stripped you before putting you in a filthy bed that was on par with torture. It wasn't his bedroom at home. Dawn Alice had had everything done in some putrid shade of pink and tried to convince him to use the word *coral* when he bitched about it, which he did often. The scuzzy Flamingo Motel was a damn sight better, even if it wasn't the Hilton. It had come with some tasty perks.

He wondered where Jaylee was. After finding the room empty and him gone, she'd probably been real pissed. Bounced out on her lovely buttocks, calling him all sorts of ugly names. Driven away from the motel in a full-fledged snit that wouldn't have eased for fifty miles. She was in Little Rock by now. He was nowhere. He wanted her to smother down on him like a warm blanket and do things to make him feel better, then bring him a tray filled with food, anything so long as it was hot and plentiful — and accompanied by a bottle of bourbon. God, even beans and cornbread or those lead-filled biscuits that could choke a catfish. He'd even eat one of Dawn Alice's unholy messes she insisted on calling French kwe-zeen.

A door slammed open. A woman came into the room, but it wasn't Dawn Alice. Not by a long shot. This woman was about the same age but also the bustiest thing he'd ever seen, her jugs braless and poking out through a ragged plaid shirt that was about three sizes too small and minus several pertinent buttons. Big ripe nipples looked back at him through the paper-thin fabric. She wore dirty, khaki trousers tied up with a piece of rope, and her feet were bare despite the cold. Her face was round, set in an expression that came straight from the primeval jungle. From underneath a simian brow unblinking yellow eyes judged him. Black, oily hair hung down her back to her waist in a bizarre waterfall of leaves, twigs, and fist-sized snarls that looked like they were made of barbed wire. Everything about her was dirty, and he could actually smell her sourness over his own prominent aroma.

All in all, she was the wildest apparition he'd ever seen.

She curled a lip at him, showing two rows of sparse brown fangs. "I be Robin Buchanon," she said in a low voice that was somewhere between a growl and a purr.

Whichever it was, it scared the shit out of Robert Drake.

Hobert drove into the Pot O'Gold, a canvas hat pulled down over his ears and sunglasses settled firmly on his nose so no one would recognize him. He'd almost taken the Caddie, but he realized it was too visible, too well-known all over Stump County. He'd settled for a nondescript used car. The sunglasses were sheer inspiration, borrowed at the last minute from his secretary. They had turquoise frames with embedded rhinestones, but Ho figured they were better than nothing. Hazelette had been less than delighted to loan them out and made him swear to bring them back.

The money was in a brown paper bag on the seat next to him. Seven hundred dollars — all the cash he could put together without raising suspicion. Not enough, but maybe green and lovely enough to get the animal off his back and away from Maggody. Permanently. If it wasn't enough, he'd have to think of something else.

The Pot O'Gold was quiet, populated only by a group of children at play in a drainage ditch and a few mangy dogs sniffing around the rows of garbage cans. Despite the crisp autumn air, Ho was sweating copiously, forced to use his handkerchief every few seconds to blot his forehead or wipe the back of his neck. He thought he'd have a little more sympathy for the Christians the next time the preacher started harping on the Romans and their recreations. Carl shared a common ancestry with slabbering lions.

There was a police car parked in front of the mobile home next to the back fence. Ho braked at a cautious distance and stared, unable to understand the unexpected wrinkle. Had Carl been nabbed in the hideout? Would he subsequently blab everything just to stir up trouble? Was there anything to do about it, to save the damp skin of the best-known car dealer in the county?

The children skipped up to the car window and asked for money to buy candy. Ho snarled at them to beat it, then sank back in the plastic upholstery to come up with an idea. The children waited on the far side of the ditch, enchanted by the visitor whose face was more colors than a watercolor set.

Dawn Alice put the pitcher of martinis on

the glass-and-chrome coffee table, which was centered on a plush white rug in front of a massive white sofa with dozens of brightly striped cushions arranged for the most festive look. She tugged at the strap of her negligee, pretending her shoulder had an itch that couldn't be resisted. It wasn't her shoulder that was itching, however, she told herself with a lazy smile.

Her hair looked immaculate, all soft and golden from a session at the beauty salon. Her toenails were pink, her fingernails scarlet and shiny, as if they were permanently wet. The negligee was her favorite color, a deep coral that gave her complexion a touch of blushing pink, and her slippers straight from Cinderella's closet, although they'd cost her quite a bit more. All in all, she matched the decor of the bedroom, which was the whole idea.

She moved the pitcher an inch to the left and stepped back to assess the scene. Tiny quiches and darling little cheese biscuits topped with pecan halves, because men liked something substantial to eat. A bowl of fruit, the grapes artfully arranged to look the most tempting (Dawn Alice had wet dreams about peeled grapes). Two chilled glasses. Candles all around the room, prepared to be lit at the perfect moment. It all looked quite nice, casual yet elegant. Exactly how she saw herself, even when she was galloping around the tennis court or doing the obligatory stint in the sauna to open her pores.

The only thing missing was a crackling fire in the gray stone fireplace. Dawn Alice lifted her demure chin and gazed through the doorway that led to the kitchen.

"Roseanna!" she roared. "Get off your butt and make a fire in here!"

An elderly Mexican woman scurried into the living room, a dish towel clutched in her reddened hands. "Yes, Miss Dawn Alice."

Dawn Alice draped herself on one end of the sofa as she watched the servant put several logs in the fireplace. There was something about a fire that heated things up, she thought smugly, imagining the fire she intended to ignite later that night.

"Is there any word on Mr. Drake?" Roseanna asked timidly, on her knees in front of the fireplace.

Dawn Alice chewed on her lower lip as she tried to remember. "Yeah, somebody or other called earlier today. A cop from Little Rock called Mr. Drake's office, and they called me. They're still looking and they have an idea where my husband is being held captive. I swear, this kidnapping is giving me migraines day and night, and I'm so sick of all those fucking telephone calls that I'm about to curl up and die. I can't believe the son of a bitch is putting me through this ordeal."

"Very sad, Miss Dawn Alice. Will there be anything else?"

"Put some of the canapés on a tray in the kitchen, then you and the other girls can take the night off. Go see one of those Mexican-speaking movies or eat some tamales with your amigos. Get yourselves laid by a Chicano stud, as long as you don't bring any lice or diseases back with you."

"Thank you, Miss Dawn Alice."

Feeling regally munificent, Dawn Alice dismissed the maid with a flip of her wrist and snuggled down among the pillows to wait. Maybe they'd work on the forearm grip tonight, although she still had trouble with her back-hand grip. Ricco did seem to enjoy helping her perfect the placement of her fingers.

"Jacks to open, trips to win," Larry Joe announced. He pushed a chip to the middle of the table. "Progressive ante."

"How many jacks to open what?" I asked, maybe sounding a tad irritable. It wasn't going exactly as I'd planned. My stacks of chips (yes, I'd bought some more) were dwindling at an alarming rate, and I hadn't won a pot in a long time.

The intricacies of the new game were explained, although it seemed silly to me. We pushed chips into the pot, drew cards, pushed in some more chips, got more cards, and basically continued in that vein for about five minutes. Eventually we watched Roy take all the chips. He had a lot more chips in front of him, most of them mine. Plover was doing all right, and looking pleased with himself. Larry Joe wasn't bitching, either.

It was my deal. I anted a chip, then shuffled the cards and beamed. "We're going to play my favorite game. Basically, it's a seven-card stud game, but with a few additions to make it more fun. That okay with everyone?" After a moment of silence, I continued. "Now threes are wild, and so are fours – but only if you pay a nickel. If the queen of spades shows up, everyone passes two cards to the left, and nines cost a dime. Well, let's make nines cost a quarter." I noticed they were looking a bit confused as I listed the rest of the rules, but hell – I'd been playing their stupid games.

Plover gave me a grin. "This one of the dorm games?"

"Why do you think that?"

He tipped back his chair and half-closed his

eyes as the grin spread. "Just a wild guess, Chief?"

"As long as we're not on duty you can call me Arly," I said sweetly, wondering if he would return the favor.

"My pleasure," murmured the Nameless Wonder. "Want another beer — Arly?"

Roy flapped his hand at me. "Let me see if I've got this straight. If I pay a quarter, then my nines are wild? Are my fours still wild, too?"

"If I get the queen of spades, do I choose which cards to pass?" Larry Joe asked, visibly bewildered.

"You'll catch on," I said with a sigh.

Carl yanked the curtain back so roughly that it ripped. Behind him on the sofa, one of the women gasped, but he kept his eyes on the road. No Cadillac coming between the mobile homes, no delivery boy trotting up the walk with a package for Carl Withers.

"I'm a going to rip that turkey's tail feathers off," he said in a low growl.

"You're expecting a turkey?" Estelle said in a voice damn snippy for someone in a rather awkward situation. "Why don't we call Boullerangelo's Wholesale Poultry Parts over in Starley City and see if they have any extras." She dabbed her forehead with a tissue she'd discovered earlier between the cushions, then passed it to Ruby Bee. It was a treasure, since there weren't any boxes of tissue in the bathroom or bedroom. "Paulie will be right pleased to pick it up for you."

The deputy nodded disjointedly. "Sure, Carl, glad to do an errand for you. I could be back in, say, thirty minutes –"

"Shut up afore I cut out your tongue and make you eat it." God, they kept babbling at him so much he couldn't keep a thought in his head. And it was real critical to figure out what to do. He couldn't hang around the Pot O'Gold much longer, not with the state police and the sheriff's boys all beating the bushes for him. He was going to have to hole up somewhere else, he decided as he jerked off the rest of the tattered curtain and dropped it on the floor to grind under his heel.

But what to do with Wynken, Blynken, and Nod? He could snuff them, and if he used the knife, real quietly, but he realized that would only get everybody more riled up and eager to get him. It might be smart to have a hostage, maybe even three, so that he could dispose of them along the way to underline his demands.

A haven came to mind, a place so remote no one would ever think to search for him there. Hell, the government men had never found the place after six years of searching for it. Only the old Maggody boys knew how to find it on Saturday night when it was too late to buy beer at the Kwik-Screw or make a run to the county line, or when they were so ornery and drunk none of the sluts in the poolhall would take them. And the Maggody boys didn't talk to the revenuers, except with broken beer bottles and upraised pool cues. Splitting heads and kicking ass.

Carl smiled, remembering the good old days before he'd taken the rap. He then turned around and showed his teeth to his hostages. "We're going to take a ride, assholes. I accidentally went and left my limousine at the prison, so I guess we'd better take the police car. If'n you're real good, maybe we can turn on the siren and bubble, and all play policeman once we get out of town. Won't that be fun?" He twirled a finger and made a whining noise, but somehow it didn't sound like all that much fun to the three on the sofa.

"Royal flush," Plover said, spreading his cards.

"Read 'em and weep," I said, doing the same. "I've got seven aces." I scooped up the mountain of chips and started putting them in neat little stacks of red, white, and blue, just like the

American flag. Poker was turning out to be fun, once we played games that required imagination. I'd have to suffer through the dull ones until it was my deal again, but I was sure I could remember some of the other games from the late-night sessions in the dorm. There was one that required the first person to get a jack to yell out something; I was sure it'd come to me in the next few minutes . . .

Plover opened his mouth. Then, sighing faintly, he closed it.

"Adultery is wicked," Mrs. Jim Bob said for the hundredth time, or so it seemed to Jim Bob as he woodenly listened to the inspired words of the saintly Reverend Willard Verber, as quoted by his wife. "The Good Book doesn't mince words on it — it says, 'Thou shall not commit adultery.' Brother Verber said last Sunday morning, from the pulpit, that adulterers were going to hell on an express train with no stops along the track of eternal damnation. I thought you were listening, Jim Bob Buchanon, listening and feeling righteous when you joined in the hymns of praise and the prayers."

She kept on gabbing, but he closed her off and tried to decide what to do about the godawful mess he and the town council were in, about waist level and rising. Fiff, the traitorous bastard, would have a reservation on Verber's express train right up front in the locomotive, if Jim Bob had any influence in that matter.

Not that he figured he did.

He wondered if Larry Joe and Roy had found Drake and put him in the back room of the trailer. Drake would probably be grateful to be rescued from the woods, and maybe, if they could jolly him up with a jar or two of hooch and a little pussy, he might agree to say he hadn't been kidnapped at all, that he'd decided of his own free will to stay at the Flamingo and later go to the deer camp for a couple of nights of poker. If they got him real drunk, he might even sign something to that effect. Jim Bob brightened, then caught his wife's glare, and resumed a penitent expression.

"Just thinking of the wisdom the good Brother Verber shares with us," he murmured, wiggling down in the chair and shaking his head to show he was beginning to feel the depth of his sinful ways.

Mrs. Jim Bob took a breath and went on, while he returned to his plan. Not an especially good one, he admitted to himself, but better than anything the other conspirators could come up with. He'd have to remind them a lot that they were in it with him, that all four of them would share the blame if they were arrested.

He knew where to get hooch strong enough to flatten a mountain cat. It wasn't cheap, but it had a mighty fine way of burning holes in your gullet all the way down and landing like a lump of napalm. It hadn't killed anybody in more than a year, that he'd heard about. As for the pussy, it went with the hooch. It was cheap, due to the filth and stink you had to fight with all the way. You had to do some other fighting, too, which Jim Bob usually enjoyed, although afterward he tried not to dwell on it too much. There was something strange about Robin Buchanon. It wasn't anything he could put his thumb on, but whatever it was kind of scared him.

"And with a common barmaid!" Mrs. Jim Bob sputtered. "That makes it all the worse. Jaylee Withers was married, too, as you full well know, and should have stayed loyal even while her cur of a husband was in prison. The Good Book says women ought to wait for their men, and follow them just like Ruth did. Brother Verber doesn't take any truck in women that want to get married but then refuse to say the vows where it makes them promise to love, honor, and obey. What you did with her was triple adultery, Jim Bob Buchanon!" She shook a finger at him (three times, he noted), sucked in another lungful of pious air, and started in again.

He considered Jaylee's untimely death. She deserved it, the scheming little bitch that she was. He'd been enjoying her favors for a long time, giving her bits of costume jewelry or candy when he felt like it or even taking her into Farberville to eat in fancy restaurants where they brought the food to the table and left the bill on a damn fool little tray. She'd adored it, and he'd appreciated her gratitude afterward, sometimes while they drove back to Maggody. It sure had shortened the drive.

But the dumb bitch had gotten herself knocked up, as if she were some junior-high-school girl who believed in divine intervention. Imagine telling him that birth-control pills were dangerous, and dropping the information after it was a damn sight too late. She didn't want an abortion, she'd simpered while she was packing. Brother Verber said abortion was a sin, and she wasn't about to incur the everlasting fires of hell when she didn't have to. All Jim Bob had to do was give her enough money to have the baby, pay a sitter while she went to the cosmetology school, and pay child support for the next eighteen years. That was all. No sweat for the rich owner of the Kwik-Screw.

He was getting angrier the more he thought about it. He hadn't paid, of course, and had laughed real loud as he left her mobile home, making sure she realized he wouldn't fall for her blackmail scheme. He'd told her to tell it all – hell, put it on the front page of the weekly newspaper right next to the obits. He'd also threatened to kill her, but she deserved it and he didn't think anybody could have heard him. Might be uncomfortable if they did, considering what happened that same night. His face was heating up when the door opened.

Mrs. Jim Bob stopped in midword and smiled at the visitor. "Thank you so much for coming, Brother Verber. As I suspected, Jim Bob's soul is in peril from the wicked path he's been on, and I wanted you to help us in our hour of need." She turned beady eyes on Jim Bob, who had slid a good six inches further down in his chair. "Aren't we lucky Brother Verber has come to pray with us?" It wasn't exactly a question.

Jim Bob managed a nod. "Real lucky. I could feel my soul on the edge of the pit, Brother Verber."

"Then let us kneel together right here on the floor and pray for guidance," Brother Verber intoned through his nose, smiling benevolently at the sinner. He could see that Satan was present, hovering in the dark corners of the room and licking his chops at the poor soul on the edge of the pit. They were going to have to roll up their sleeves and wrestle with the devil. Brother Verber was inspired by the possibilities, and he felt a good, old-fashioned, knee-breaking prayer coming on.

TWELVE

Hobert Middleton gaped over the steering wheel at the procession emerging from Jaylee's mobile home. It was about the most peculiar thing he'd seen in a long time, and way beyond making any sense. Estelle came first, goose-stepping like a Nazi and rigid with anger. She was followed by Ruby Bee, who looked like she was on the brink of a coronary, her face white and her steps jerky and wobbly. Then Paulie Buchanon, staring at the sidewalk and barely able to stumble along, despite Carl Withers right on his heels. Carl was the only one who looked as if he was enjoying the parade to the police car. In fact, Ho mused in perplexity, Carl looked downright delighted with himself.

Paulie and Ruby Bee got in the front seat; the other two exchanged words, then climbed in back. Carl stuck a gun in the back of Paulie's neck, snarled something else to Estelle, and then wiggled down so far Ho could see only an oily circle of hair. The police car maneuvered around and slowly drove toward Ho, who came to his senses at the last minute and ducked down below the wheel, bumping his nose along the way.

When he rose cautiously, the police car was easing over the cattle guard. He was surprised when it turned away from the highway and headed toward the bridge and the road that wound through the national forest for at least fifty miles before meeting up with another state highway. He mopped his neck one last time, gingerly touched his nose to see if it was bleeding (it wasn't, but it still hurt), then started his car and drove after them at what he hoped was a prudent distance. As he slowed down at the cattle guard, he flipped the sunglasses out the car window.

"You have to yell 'Jack Sprat,' or someone else can take the card," I explained patiently for the third time. They were having a hard time grasping the game, and not, I suspected, putting their minds to it with any great diligence. They'd made me play all kinds of unfamiliar games; I saw no reason for them to balk at mine. Balk like pie-eyed mules, I might add.

"Jack Sprat!" I yelled, demonstrating in case it still hadn't sunk in.

"Jack Sprat," Plover said. He looked around the table.

"Jack Sprat," Larry Joe and Roy echoed obediently, although not with enough enthusiasm to frost a cupcake.

I told them the rest of the rules, dealt a few cards, then stopped. "Let me see one more time if I've got this straight. Jim Bob called the emergency meeting last night at eight o'clock, right? Then you put Drake in the trunk of Ho's car, and you two went to your respective homes to pack and meet behind the Kwik-Screw at ten o'clock. What'd Jim Bob and Ho do?"

Roy lifted a corner of his card, no doubt prepared to yell out the appropriate words should he discover a jack. He lowered it with a disappointed expression. "Ho said he had to meet somebody at his lot. He didn't sound very happy at the prospect, so it wasn't some good old boy looking for a new station wagon for the wife. He said he'd keep Drake in the trunk for the time being. Jim Bob said he was going to run an errand, then go home to collect some food."

"How'd he look?" I asked.

"About as nervous as a long-tailed cat in a room full of rocking chairs. Right pissed, too, now that I think on it."

I thought about the various paths for a minute, then glanced at Plover. "Either one of those two could have gone to Jaylee's trailer and arranged to meet her at the motel, although I sure as hell don't know why. Did Jaylee know you'd transferred Drake to the trunk?"

Roy shook his head. "We did it right quick, before any of us could chicken out and hightail it for the state line. I don't think anybody saw us. Ho drove right up to the door of Number Three, and it only took a minute or two to fetch Drake because he already had his stuff in his suitcase."

"Why was that?" Plover said. Interrupted, I thought to myself, but I settled for a frown, since it was pretty close to what I was going to say anyway.

"I don't reckon we asked him. He was squawking like a guinea hen, so we just kind of stuffed him in the trunk and closed the lid to save having to listen to him."

"I'll bet Jaylee planned to pick him up on her way out of town," I said to Plover. "That's why he was all packed and ready to leave. They probably worked up the scheme earlier in the day, as soon as she found out she'd passed the GED and was headed for fame and glory in the big city. I wonder if anybody else knew?"

"Don't see how they could," Roy murmured. "Drake didn't have a telephone in the room or in the trunk of the Caddie, so he sure couldn't have told anybody. It'd be right stupid of Jaylee to announce it."

"If Jim Bob went to her place to discuss the pregnancy, she might have told him," I said, still frowning hard enough to leave etch marks on my forehead. Ruby Bee is telling me all the time I'll be sorry later, when I look like someone drew a road map above my eyebrows. It isn't my most worrisome concern. "But he knew Drake wasn't at the motel anymore. I guess he might have allowed her to think otherwise, then waited for her to come. Let her look inside Number Three for Drake, then caught her as she came out the door."

"The motive being blackmail?" Plover said, his forehead headed for the same fate as mine, atlas-style. "She demanded a payoff to keep quiet about the affair and its unmissable proof, and he said he'd bring the money to the motel?"

Larry Joe and Roy were puffing and goggling as we talked, so I assumed they weren't up to date on Jim Bob's extramarital activities. Poker table bragging wasn't as prevalent as I'd thought, at least not in Maggody circles. I wasn't in the mood to enlighten them.

"The problem is that I can't imagine Jaylee telling him she was going to steal Drake from under his nose," I said. "She'd realize he wouldn't let her do it, because that would get the chummy conspirators in bad trouble." I glared at the two of them to let them know I hadn't forgotten what they'd done to my mother, then went on. "Jim Bob wasn't about to let Drake slip away until he called Fiff, and he couldn't do that until today. I don't see why she'd let out one little peep about the plan, so how would he know to ambush her later at the motel?"

"Inspired guess?" Plover suggested. "Or maybe she blurted out something while she was angry."

I grimaced as I considered the scenario. Having never been present at a blackmail conference, I didn't know for sure how the dialogue was likely to go.

"No," I said slowly, "you didn't know Jaylee. She was blond and built like a beauty queen, but she had a sharp mind and she was too damn cunning to let someone out if she thought it'd backfire. She was looking out for Number One. As delightful as the possibility is, I don't know how Jim Bob could have murdered her."

"How about the husband, then? From the

prison report, I gathered Carl Withers's a real mean one who wouldn't hesitate to murder a total stranger, much less his wife. When I checked in earlier, I asked if there'd been any updates on him. Nobody has the foggiest notion where he is right now."

"According to Jaylee, he's three-quarters of the way to the Gulf of Mexico. I don't think he'd be bullheaded enough to come north after his escape, but even if he did, how would he know Jaylee would be at the Flamingo Motel? And where would he get a crossbow?"

"Carl liked to hunt with them, and I know for a fact he bought a new one three years ago," Larry Joe volunteered. "He used to come by the shop to show me what was left of the coons and squirrels after he'd shot them. It did some right nasty damage, on account of their size."

It had done the same to Jaylee, I remembered with a shudder. "So he could have gotten his crossbow from the mobile home, I suppose. But that doesn't explain why he'd know to hang out behind the motel, waiting for Jaylee to come."

We pondered that one for a few minutes, each of us competing to come up with an answer. The Nameless Wonder won, or at least he thought he did.

"Maybe he was outside the mobile home and

overheard Jim Bob and Jaylee when they had the conversation about blackmail. That would rile any husband to murder. Then he followed Jaylee to the motel and shot her in a jealous rage."

"If he was following her, when did he get his paws on the crossbow?" I said with great reason. "Are you suggesting he knocked on the door beforehand and politely asked to use the potty, then slipped out with the crossbow under his coat? I can't imagine Jaylee handling that without doing something – like calling the police. She was terrified of Carl."

"He got the crossbow from somewhere else," Plover replied. "You said everybody in town owns one. He just stole it from the back of someone's truck."

"And jogged down the highway after Jaylee's car, which doesn't qualify for the Indy 500 but can go at a reasonable speed? I gave her a ticket once for doing seventy miles per hour through the school zone. She said her hair was falling down in back and it was an emergency. Believed it, too."

"He stole a car." Sergeant Plover seemed a shade irritated by my unassailable logic; his eyes were thunderclouds and his ears flushed darker than pansy petals. His face glowed like a fluorescent lamp. "Happens all the time."

"Why don't you call home and see if there are any possible stolen vehicles?" I said demurely, basking in his heat. I tilted my head to get an even tan and added, "While you're at it, ask Paulie if he could run over to Jaylee's mobile home to search for the crossbow. I don't see how Carl could have gotten it, but it would help to know if it's there or not."

He stood up abruptly, managing to jar the table hard enough to topple my tidy stacks of chips. As he stomped out the door, a snarl drifted back to us. It sounded like "Jack Sprat," but I could have been wrong.

Jim Bob's kneecaps ached like they'd never ached before. Brother Verber was making inroads with the devil, but progress was slow and methodical, with a lingering stop at each sin to give it careful attention. It occurred to Jim Bob that the repentance might take longer than the sin, although Jaylee hadn't ever complained. He opened one eye in a squint and caught Mrs. Jim Bob staring at him. He quickly closed his eye, wiggled around a bit to ease the pain, and tried to decide how best to get out of there before they had to wheel him over to some hospital for crippled people and amputees.

"Amen," Brother Verber announced, hanging on to the final sound until Jim Bob and Mrs.

Jim Bob joined in.

"Thank you kindly, Brother Verber," Jim Bob said as he staggered to his feet. "It's a great comfort to know my soul is no longer in danger of eternal damnation. I feel so secure that I want to give you a check for the church building fund or those dear little hungry children of Africa."

Brother Verber rocked back on his toes and smoothly arose, his knees apparently conditioned to such sieges. "Any contribution will be appreciated, Brother Buchanon, but we aren't finished yet. I haven't even started on the way you lied to your fine Christian wife here, or helped you to cleanse the filth from your lustful carnal organs by allowing you to admit each and every time you engaged in adultery. We're going to listen to all the shameful details so we can pray over them. No, Brother Buchanon, your soul is still in terrible trouble. I can hear Satan smacking his lips as he puts your name in his book of lost souls. I'm just taking a break so's I can wet my whistle with pure, sparkling water."

Mrs. Jim Bob stood up and joined the preacher in the doorway. "You have a lot more confessing to do, Jim Bob; you might want a glass of water yourself." She took Verber's arm and patted it. "We're so lucky to have you on call, Brother Verber. Are you sure you wouldn't rather have an RC cola and a bag of peanuts?"

Jim Bob made an obscene gesture at the door as it swung closed. Verber sounded like he intended to rant for the next twelve hours. Mrs. Jim Bob most likely had some additional comments to make, if Verber ever ran out of righteousness. God, he'd be in the office on his knees until the two figured out how to make hell freeze over out of boredom.

Ho had promised to show up more than an hour ago so they could drive back to the deer camp. Where the fuck was Ho? How was he, the leader of the goddamn incompetents, supposed to do anything when everybody sat on the pot with a magazine all damn day?

Dahlia opened the door, her ponderous chin aquiver with curiosity. "Mrs. Jim Bob suggested you might want to use the facilities before you recommence praying. She said to tell you it's going to be a mighty long session in your struggle with the devil."

Jim Bob curled his fingers, but an idea saved Dahlia from his wrath. "That's a fine suggestion of Mrs. Jim Bob's, don't you think? That way I won't be distracted on the road to blessed salvation. By the way, has Hobert Middleton come by as of yet?"

"I ain't seen him, but you could ask Kevin."

Dahlia thudded away for the candy rack. Delivery work always made her hungry.

Jim Bob went to the front of the store, ignoring his wife and Brother Verber in the aisle in front of the soda pop display case. Kevin was taping a piece of paper to the glass door. Jim Bob snatched it away and wadded it up, snarling, "What do you think you was about to do, you lump of sheep shit? This ain't no bulletin board — it's a service station."

Kevin put the tape behind his back. "Raz asked me to stick it up somewheres where everybody would read it. It tells about Betty's memorial service and funeral on Thursday. From the description, it ought to be right pretty. Hymns and everything."

Jim Bob thought of several things to say, all of them unpleasant and involving convolutions of paternity. But there wasn't time, and Kevin wouldn't understand half of them anyway. "Don't put anything on the door if you value your prick," he said mildly, stuffing the wadded paper in his pocket. "You and the cow will have to work late tonight and lock up; I got other things to do."

He hurried to the men's room and locked the door behind him. Steeling himself not to think how idiotic he looked, he climbed onto the toilet, opened the window, and squirmed through the narrow opening. It was a ten-foot drop, he figured, and onto discarded tires and a pile of empty oil cans. He'd take his chances with a broken leg — which would be a damn sight more entertaining than another session with Verber and the devil.

If he survived, he thought he'd better hustle up to Robin's for a couple of mason jars of white lightning. Another ten bucks and she'd agree to come to the trailer to screw Drake in the back room. While they waited, Roy could write up some legal-sounding paper that said Drake hadn't been kidnapped. After the hooch and Robin Buchanon, Drake would sign anything. Hell, he'd never know what hit him.

Plover came back in the trailer and slammed the door. "No wonder your deputy didn't get in the state police academy. He couldn't get in the regular academy, either, since he doesn't even understand how to operate a police band."

"It doesn't work most of the time," I said, "so don't you start making cracks about Officer Buchanon. He works extra shifts all the time, and usually comes in early to help me with the paperwork. He'd make a better state trooper than some I could mention if I had a mind to." Clarence Darrow, were you listening?

"The radio's working just fine!" Plover

snapped. "The problem is that your deputy has a woman with him, and she can't figure out which knobs to turn, so she cut me off in the middle of a sentence. It's probably some little high-school girl who hasn't learned to read as of yet."

"That's a crock if I ever heard one! Officer Buchanon wouldn't have a girl in his unit unless she was a witness."

"Witnessing what — the way his fly opens and closes? From what I heard, she was right breathless with admiration."

I flicked my eyes down, then gave him a sugary smile. "More than some folks can say." I let him seethe on that one while I tried to think what Paulie might be up to. Nothing came to mind, so I tucked it away and said, "I presume you had more success with the county dispatcher. What'd she say?"

"The sheriff and posse are out looking for Drake, but they hadn't seen any sign of him. They haven't bumped into Carl Withers, either, although they're watching for him. You may be right that he's gone south."

"I thought we was going to play cards," Roy said, toying with his chips. "I think I understand the game, and I want to see."

Larry Joe asked him a question about wild cards. I left them to discuss the issue and looked at Plover. "Let's see if we can figure out where everybody was between eight and ten o'clock. The answer's in there somewhere, but it's murkier than mud pie stew. There's only one thing I know for sure — and that's what happened to Raz Buchanon's dog."

Roy hushed Larry Joe. "Did Perkins admit he stole her? Did you arrest him?"

"The case of the purloined hound?" Plover said, trying not to laugh (he did that a lot).

"Raz was very fond of Betty," I said. "He was in last week to report the theft, and filed a report and everything. It may seem a trifle to you, but it was important to him."

"My apologies, Chief." He sat down and locked his hands behind his head. "Tell me about the case — I'm fascinated by police procedure in your department. Maybe we can use some of your techniques in the state office."

Roy was still eager to hear, so I told them about Betty's unseemly fate on the highway, even using Raz's poetic description of the body at the scene of the crime. Roy looked downcast, and Larry Joe had to swallow a couple of times to maintain his composure. Plover wasn't visibly distressed, but he had the decency to close his eyes in a brief moment of respect for the fallen warrior. I was sort of touched, myself.

After a silence, I said, "So we know where

Betty was on Sunday night – the middle of the highway. Larry Joe and Roy say they were home packing to come up here; I'll have to investigate their alibis when we get back to town." I gave that a minute to sink in, then continued. "Jaylee left about eight o'clock to pack her things, and I'm assuming she planned to sneak behind the motel around ten to pick up Drake. Drake we know about. Estelle and Ruby Bee were busy with the guests who weren't ready to leave until closing time." I stopped for a nose count. "Jim Bob and Ho were off somewhere. Jim Bob's got the best motive, but I'm not convinced he did it, and Ho doesn't have any motive that I know of. That leaves Carl, who may be in Baton Rouge."

"You skipped somebody," Plover said quietly. "When a husband indulges in an illicit affair, there's another party involved."

"Mrs. Jim Bob?" I said, thinking he'd lost his mind.

Plover shifted his eyes across the table. "Or Joyce Lambertino."

Larry Joe began to cough and sputter protests, his jerky hands sending chips everywhere in a plastic clatter. Roy muttered something about the call of nature and hurried outside. I sat back to stare.

Brother Verber sank to his knees outside the locked door of the men's room. "I know you're feeling mighty blue right now, Brother Jim Bob," he said loudly. "You're in there because you want to be alone while you ponder the evil things you've done. I'm going to let you stay there inside them four cold walls, but I want you to know I'm here with you as your spiritual coach."

Mrs. Jim Bob wasn't convinced, but she didn't want to contradict Brother Verber or do anything to spoil his tempo. Tightening her lips, she knelt behind the rump of the reverend and clasped her hands together. "I'm here, too," she said loud enough to be heard in the laundromat next door. "You'd better be in there, Jim Bob Buchanon, on your knees and ready for redemption."

Brother Verber took off like a 747 aimed for Europe, his voice full of melodious, booming threats that would scare the horns off Satan, if he was listening.

Mrs. Jim Bob relaxed as the voice washed over her. She decided she'd done the right thing, after all, although it had sorely tried her soul. The Withers woman had been a slut; Brother Verber had readily agreed when she'd first told him of Jim Bob's sinfulness several months ago. Sluts didn't deserve any pity or forgiveness, even if they attended church every Sunday and Wednesday and taught Sunday school as if they were righteous, God-fearing Christian housewives. Sluts deserved whatever they got. Mrs. Jim Bob figured God knew that, too. She clasped her hands a little more tightly and silently threw in a good word for herself, just in case God had missed any of the explanation.

"Amen," she whispered to Brother Verber's rump.

Roy came back in, zipping up his pants. "Your radio's crackling like it was on fire," he told Plover.

He looked at me as he scrambled to his feet. "Maybe they found something in the woods. You want to come listen, too?"

We all four hustled outside and gathered around the jeep. Larry Joe was still white and shaky, but I didn't have much sympathy for him since I'd learned he was visiting Jaylee after he mopped the high school. Would have been nice if somebody had thought to tell me before. He denied having stopped by after he left home the previous night, but we weren't buying.

Plover did some knob-twisting and barking into the microphone. Through the static the dispatcher said that one of the posse members had stumbled onto a cabin in the woods that seemed right suspicious. Not too far from where we were, but not on their map. Something unclear about a shotgun and some resulting injury to the posse member's backside. We all sucked in some air and waited through another blizzard of static, but the voice faded.

I hit my fist into my hand. "Good Lord, Sergeant Plover, don't you know how to operate a simple radio?" I took the survey map out of the jeep and hurried inside to see if I could figure out where the cabin might be located.

The others joined me, one of them looking miffed. I traced several of the lines that zigzagged through the mountains, trying to guess which one passed a cabin I'd never heard of. At last I jabbed my finger down. "This road, maybe. But who the hell lives out in the middle of nowhere and would be likely to put a load of buckshot in a stranger's rear end?"

Roy, Larry Joe, and I exchanged looks. "Robin Buchanon," we mouthed in unison, unconsciously whispering out of some innate awe at the very name.

"Who's that?" Plover demanded. "Would Drake take sanctuary with her? Can we drive to her cabin without going all the way back to the highway?"

After studying the map, I found a road that ran across the top of the ridge. We put on our coats and went to the jeep. Plover was still asking questions about Robin Buchanon, but nobody could find the precise words to describe her.

THIRTEEN

Ruby Bee stared at the radio, too frightened to touch it but wishing it would do something again, if only to give her a false sense of security. She went so far as to lift her hand, but a growl from the backseat stopped her.

"Who you want to talk to, old lady?" Carl grunted.

"I was aiming to scratch my nose," she said haughtily. "But if it makes you nervous, I'll just let it itch."

"Right jumpy, ain't you?" Estelle added.

"Maybe you two broads would like to find out how itchy my trigger finger is," Carl said. He waved the gun under the redhead's nose, but he didn't have much heart in it. The car bounced along like a drop of water on a hot skillet, and his ankle hurt real bad. He hadn't decided what he was going to do with his hostages once they got to Robin's cabin or what he was going to do with himself, either. Robin was good for a jar of hooch, a mess of chitterlings, and an imaginative screw, but then what?

"There's a road up ahead," Paulie said through clenched teeth. "Am I supposed to turn?"

Carl scratched his crotch with the gun while he tried to remember. It seemed to help. "Yeah, asshole, turn there. It's about two, three miles that way, I think."

"I demand to know where you're taking us."

The redhead, of course. God, his ears was tired of her bitching and complaining. If he had to snuff a hostage, she was going to get the first bullet, about an inch above her ear. He gave her a warning growl and draped over the top of the front seat to make sure the asshole turned the right way.

"Switch on the radio again," he ordered the other broad. "See if we can hear what the sheriff's got in mind. I think I'm going to get myself one of these things so I can listen to the fuzzboys when they talk to each other. Come in right handy when you've a mind to avoid them."

Ruby Bee peeked at Paulie, but he kept his eyes straight ahead. A nerve jumped on his jaw, the only sign of life on his otherwise icy face. He didn't look like he was going to show her which button to twist anytime soon. The last time she'd fiddled with the knobs in response to the terse demands coming out of the box, she'd felt the shadow of death breathing over her shoulder. Sighing, she chose the closest one.

"Officer Buchanon, are you there? Can you hear me?"

"That's Arly!" Ruby Bee shrieked. "Did you hear that, Estelle? Arly's on the radio trying to find Paulie! Hey, Paulie, why don't you answer her and tell her what's happening?"

A gun barrel tapped her on the cheek. "I ain't sure that's a smart idea," Carl said, swearing under his breath. Amateurs! "This Arly might decide to tell the sheriff where we was, and I wouldn't be real pleased if'n that happened. I know you broads don't understand right well, but I am what's called an escaped convict."

"Then you shouldn't have broken the law in the first place," Estelle said. "Law-abiding citizens don't go to prison, and they therefore don't find theirselves obliged to escape from it."

Carl toyed with the idea of shooting off the tip of her nose, but he doubted that would shut her up. He settled for a backhand across her face, which produced a muffled snort of outrage. "You don't know the half of it, lady. I didn't do nothing to get the rap — except make a little deal with a shit-faced wimp too scared to piss in his pants."

"You got drunk, stole a car, ran down a child, and subsequently totaled the vehicle," Paulie muttered. "I remember the case, even though I wasn't a deputy at the time. You pleaded guilty and tried to bargain yourself out of it, but it was your third DWI in less than a year."

The radio crackled once more. "Officer Buchanon, are you there?"

Carl ground the barrel into Paulie's neck, smiling at the red circle it left. "You count real good, Deputy Dawg. Turn off that goddamn radio before I let you count your brains on the windshield, and you other two just shut your traps and give a man some peace and quiet." He twisted the barrel once more for good measure.

The radio was turned off. The car bounced along the rutted road toward the cabin.

Hobert turned on the poor excuse for a road, wondering where the hell they were going. Cotton's Ridge lay a mile or so to the west, but there wasn't anything in the direction they went, unless you liked to look at scrub oaks and stunted fir trees. He slowed down to a crawl and frowned at the woods that closed in on both sides like tattered curtains. It was getting late in the afternoon, and a mite dark. Colder, too, and the heater didn't do more than grumble.

If the car in front turned around for some reason and came back, he was up shit creek without a paddle. If he came to a fork, there wasn't any way of telling which way to go in order to follow them; he'd just as well flip a coin or spit in the wind. If he inadvertently caught up with them, he might as well kill himself and save Carl the bother. The whole thing was downright stupid. Here he was the most respected car dealer in the county *(Ho, Ho, Ho Middleton for a crackerjack deal on new or used)*, hot on the trail of an escaped convict, two old ladies, and a cop with a mail-order badge.

He didn't even know why.

He was pondering his stupidity when he hit the rock in the middle of the road. The thump was loud enough to raise the dead and more than adequate to do something godawful to the tire and axle. The car lurched into a tree. After a moment of hesitation, the tree shivered like a virgin in a nightgown, then slowly toppled down across the hood of the car with a tremendous boom that seemed to echo on and on.

Ho knew enough cuss words to avoid repeating himself for the next five minutes. The trees were empty of squirrels and birds when he finally settled down and got out of the car to study the damage. There wasn't any way he could move the tree, he decided morosely, or even back out from under it. Damn axle was bent anyway, so he sure couldn't drive home for a slug of bourbon and a handful of tranquilizers. Brother Verber wasn't likely to step out from behind a rock to pray for a mechanical miracle.

After a final spray of sunlight, the sun ducked behind the mountaintop, throwing a blanket of gloom across the valley. It was right quiet; not even a jay shrilled displeasure at him from a nearby branch. Ho realized his breathing was the only sound, and it was on the unruly side. He took a few deep breaths to steady himself, then strained to hear the sound of a car in the distance. At last he heard a low moan, sporadic and whiny, way down the side of the mountain.

He looked at the way he'd come. It was a hell of a long way back to the pavement, and a good ten miles more back to Maggody. In the dark nobody was going to stop for a hitchhiker, not with an escaped convict making the television news every night. He buttoned up his coat, muttered a last unpleasantry at the car, and set off down the road in the direction he'd been going. What the hell.

As he disappeared around a bend, a child crept out of the brush. Its gender was lost under a filthy mop of shoulder-length black hair and a face lined with dirt, and it wore denim overalls that creaked with each quick movement. The feet were bare, but callused heavily enough to walk across a blackberry patch without taking any notice. Sober yellow eyes peered out from under a distorted brow. There was a sly grin on its face, since this was the first time the plan had ever worked. The others were all the time jeering, saying there was no point in putting a rock in the middle of a road nobody ever came on. They'd said it had cornmeal mush instead of brains. Five of the total of ten years had been trying to prove otherwise.

Grunting like a sow in heat, the child rolled the rock back to its rightful position, then turned to smile triumphantly at its first trophy. As it idly scratched its head, the child felt a tremor of indecision about what to do next, since the plan had never been worked out far enough to deal with success. At last the child opened the door and got into the car, prepared to remove anything that came off without too much work. The bag on the seat was impossible to miss. A waterfall of money was dumped on the seat.

"Hot goddamn motherfuckin' shit," the hunter hissed through a gap in its teeth. "The others are gonna be piss-sorry they ever laughed at me, the fuckin' bastards."

But what to do with it? Was it enough to run away and join a gang of murdering pirates? It looked like enough to buy a goddamn pirate ship like in the book (the only one ever seen), but the child had no way of counting it. Money was good to have, she always said, necessary to buy jars or bags of flour and rice. Nobody ever suggested learning to count it. She'd have offered a wallop across the side of the head or a session with a willow switch at the suggestion.

The money was crammed back in the bag, and the bag stuffed down the front of the overalls until a decision about pirates was reached. The child then climbed onto the top of the car. Opening its mouth, it let out a bloodcurdling screech of victory as two feet smashed down on the roof. Then, the others could see the footprints in the deep dent, proving the story was right true.

The child scuttled back into the brush.

Ho heard the screech drifting through the darkness behind him. The idea of a twisted ankle didn't seem so bad, and he quickened his pace.

"I think we need to turn here," I said, pointing at a narrow, weedy road that vanished into the woods. I had the map spread out in my lap, but it was getting harder to read in the dusky light, and I sure as hell didn't want to get us lost.

Sergeant Plover braked. "Let me see the map, Chief, and see if you can find a flashlight in the glove compartment. I sure as hell don't want to get us lost." Maybe his first name was Harry, as in Houdini.

Larry Joe cleared his throat. "This doesn't look like it goes anywheres, Arly. Maybe we ought to go back to the deer camp and wait for some more information from the sheriff's office."

"Robin doesn't take kindly to visitors," Roy added unhappily. "If she's already shot up one poor fool, she's liable to shoot the rest of us without even thinking about it, presuming she thinks about anything."

"Would you two like to get out right here and walk back?" I said as I dug through the glove compartment. "It's not more than five miles back, and you ought to be a third of the way there before it gets completely dark and the bears come out. They're hungry in the fall, but that shouldn't scare you brave old boys."

I found a light. Plover and I studied the map, me pointing to the narrow line. "That's it," I said in a voice that sounded a whale of a lot more confident than I felt. "It appears to be less than three miles, as long as we don't belly onto a log and get caught."

"This Buchanon woman actually lives there?" he said. He didn't sound as if my attempt at confidence had been real successful. "How does she get into town?"

"She doesn't," Roy said from the backseat.

"What does she do for staples that she can't grow? And didn't you say earlier she has children? How do they get to school every day?"

"Robin Buchanon's bastards don't go to school," Roy said. "They're as wild a bunch of untamed animals as you'd ever imagine, and the school would prefer not to have them. The school board passed a special resolution saying Robin's children didn't have to ever come to school, that she could teach them herself."

"She's educated?" Plover said, bewildered.

"Depends on what you mean by educated," Roy snickered. "If you want to know the exact ingredients for white lightning or how to distill it until it's bad enough to scald a goat, Robin can tell you. She's also got some knowledge in areas I wouldn't be comfortable describing in front of a lady."

Plover cocked a thumb in my direction. "Her?"

"Yeah," I said, "I'm Eliza Dolittle and you're that professor. Are we going to sing 'The Rain in Spain' or are we going to get down this road before it gets darker than the inside of a cistern?"

Humming to himself, Plover turned on the mean road and we crept down the mountainside in what I dearly hoped was the direction of Robin Buchanon's cabin. There were several large rocks in the middle of the road, but our vigilant driver managed to avoid them.

"How about a hymn of rejoicing?" Brother Verber boomed. "I think your husband might find great spiritual comfort in it, and maybe even find the courage to come out of there and look you straight in the eye, fall to his knees, and beg your everlasting forgiveness."

Mrs. Jim Bob's lips were so tight they ached worse than her knees. It took an act of willpower to loosen them enough to speak. "If you think so, Brother Verber. But I'm worried about him being in there so long, without a peep or anything. Do you think he might have gone to sleep?"

"Wrestling with the devil has taken away his voice," Brother Verber explained genially. "I seen it before, although not with this great quantity of perseverance. Let's ask the others to join along with us, so we can send our hymn right through the door to Brother Jim Bob's heart. He'll be so gladdened he'll come out and thank us."

Mrs. Jim Bob called for Dahlia and Kevin, who'd been hovering nearby to watch the show. Dahlia thought about telling Brother Verber that Jim Bob had driven away more than fifteen minutes before, but she remembered what the preacher had said to her granny a year ago about certain events in the basement of the church during the Wednesday-night prayer meeting. The old fart.

Kevin, the apple of her eyes, took her hand as they knelt behind Mrs. Jim Bob's ramrod backside. "Just like taking vows," he whispered, squeezing her pudgy fingers until they threatened to pop.

She gave him a gentle, uncomprehending smile and aimed her crescent eyes at the pink circle on Brother Verber's head. Then, at the whispered count of three, she opened her mouth to sing Jim Bob right out of the men's room. Kevin thought she sounded just like one of those angels up in heaven. And looked like two or three of them.

Jim Bob slowed down in front of Ho's car lot, but he didn't see any sign of the dealer or salesmen. If Ho had them in the office, still kicking ass after all this time, it was too goddamn bad. He turned around on the gravel shoulder and drove toward the county road that led to Robin Buchanon's shack in the woods. He figured he had just enough time to get there before dark. He'd hustle her and her jars in the car and get to the deer camp before it was too late to pacify Drake – if Roy and Larry Joe'd found him and brought him back.

The whole goddamn mess was wearing down his soul faster than Brother Verber's nonstop sermonizing, he told himself as he passed the Kwik-Stoppe Shoppe. An icy lump plopped into his stomach as he saw Mrs. Jim Bob and Brother Verber staring at him through the plate-glass door. There wasn't anything to do but jam down the gas pedal and hope the hell they hadn't really seen him, even though he'd had a clear view of the fire in his wife's eyes.

"Aw, shit!" he muttered through his teeth as he turned by the Pot O'Gold sign and sped away from Maggody – and the wrath of God.

Mrs. Jim Bob snapped her lips together and

snatched her purse off the counter. Shoving Brother Verber into step, she hurried him out the door to her car and put him in the front seat. She then ran around to the driver's side, frantically digging through her purse for the keys, and slid behind the wheel.

"Did you see where he turned?" she growled at her passenger.

"Up there at the sign," her passenger managed to gasp. Preaching required fortitude, not haste, and he wasn't accustomed to being escorted at such a pace.

"He's headed for sin," Mrs. Jim Bob said as they drove down the highway at a terrifying speed. She gritted her teeth while she squealed around the corner, then relaxed a tad as she spotted the taillights in the distance. "I don't know where he's going, but I know it ain't to church to do some repentance at the altar. We're going to follow him all the way, Brother Verber, and catch him in the very act of evilness."

That sounded like a good idea to Brother Verber, who'd had to rely on his imagination most of his life. That and magazines, which he'd read only so he could grasp the enormity of all the sinfulness in the world and be armed with righteous knowledge of what he, personally, was up against. And the movie he'd slipped into in Little Rock, when he'd been attending a convention, had provided a heap of righteous knowledge; he'd sat through it three times to get all the details. Or was it four times?

"How'd he get out of the men's room?" Mrs. Jim Bob muttered, mostly to herself. She pulled in her lips until they formed a perfect circle of symmetrical disapproval.

Brother Verber wrenched his mind away from the cinema and took it upon himself to explain how God worked in the most puzzling ways, that sometimes God arranged for a sinner to be sorely tempted one final time before salvation was given.

"But how'd he get out of the men's room?"

Brother Verber moved on to the mysterious ways God did this kind of thing when you weren't looking. This was one of his favorite themes; he figured it would last until they got where they were going and caught Brother Jim Bob at his most degrading. The anticipation warmed Brother Verber until his voice flowed like golden honey dribbling out of an over-turned jar.

Mrs. Jim Bob curled her fingers around the steering wheel as she stared at the distant red lights.

Despite the sudden exodus of a goodly number of Maggody residents, the town was by no means devoid of life. Raz Buchanon moved up the side of the highway, pausing to nail flyers on telephone poles or to tape them on dirty glass windows that had once displayed the wares of long-gone shops. He muttered continually under his breath, with pauses only to expel tobacco juice or to wipe the tears of grief off his concave cheeks. The few other pedestrians moved out of his path, motivated by past experiences.

Down at Ruby Bee's Bar and Grill, a handful of hungry regulars stood in a group outside the locked door. Everybody agreed it was damned peculiar that nobody was there, the lights off and the inside quieter than the restrooms at the high school when the principal walked in. After a certain amount of good-natured jibes, one brave soul went around the corner to the Flamingo Motel, although he gave only a sideways peek at Number Three. He returned to report Ruby Bee wasn't home, neither. Everybody was right puzzled, but after a while they got in their trucks and drifted toward the Dairy Dee-Lishus to get something to eat.

Estelle's five o'clock appointment was downright indignant, having left work early especially to have a permanent. It was real rude of Estelle not to be there, she fumed, what with her cousin's wedding on Saturday and all. The appointment scrawled a nasty note and stuck it in the handle of the screen door. She rapped on the window once more just to be on the safe side, then puffed away to call her cousin in Starley City and relate the outrage.

Perkins saw Raz taping something on the window of Roy's antique store. He kept his eyes firmly on the yeller line as he drove past in his rusted gray truck filled with sacks of layer grit.

Joyce Lambertino put her arm over the back of the seat to slap at a whining child, but she didn't even slow down. After four children, she'd had enough experience to do it in her sleep. The grocery list was taped on the dashboard; the wad of coupons clipped together in her lap. If the children kept up the current volume of whines and squabbles, she'd be forced to buy a box of animal crackers and open it as soon as they got inside the store, although it wasn't on the budget this week. Larry Joe had told her to hold the grocery money to fifty dollars a week. She'd like to see him try to feed six mouths on that much and still buy laundry detergent and toilet paper, too. Her pleasure at the mental scene evaporated as the child on the seat next to her commenced to throw up all over the place.

Dahlia unwrapped a candy bar with one

hand, the other occupied with a bright orange Nehi can. Crinkle and whoosh, her two most favorite sounds in the whole world. Jim Bob wouldn't be back for a long time, she thought complacently. If'n Mrs. Jim Bob and the old fart ever caught him, he might never come back. Would that mean she and Kevin would get the store? She called him over and asked him what he thought.

Kevin gazed at his beloved, all those glorious pounds of her. His mouth watered as he thought about the undulating flesh beneath the blue tent, and all the ways he'd learned to make it ripple like it was in a summer breeze. Speechless with lust, he took her hand and began the arduous chore of tugging her to her feet.

"What's that?" Plover said, slamming on the brakes. "What kind of damn fool leaves a car in the middle of the road?"

"A damn fool with a tree on his car," I said. I couldn't see anyway to drive around it, so I sweetly suggested we walk the rest of the way. An objection from the backseat died when I mentioned he could wait there until we got back. With Daniel Boone Plover at the head of the line, we took off down the road.

Jim Bob was too pissed to swear as he slammed on the brakes. Goddamn fools going off somewhere and leaving their cars where other folks couldn't get around them. He dug out a flashlight from under the seat and took off down the road.

Mrs. Jim Bob felt an unnatural word spring to her lips as she slammed on the brakes. Realizing Brother Verber would never forgive her if he knew she harbored such unholy thoughts, she clamped her lips together tighter than a vise. An irritated squeak sneaked through.

"How most amazing to find these cars here," Brother Verber said, unaware of the internal struggle going on beside him. "I wonder if all these drivers are engaging in some sort of black mass or devil worship where they all get naked and partake in group sex?"

"We'd better go see," Mrs. Jim Bob said as she got out of the car, but Brother Verber was a good step ahead of her. He was taking off down the road so fast she wasn't sure she could keep up with him.

The child stood gaping at the treasure trove awaiting greedy little fingers. The money was tucked away where the others would never find

it, but here was a lot more stuff just waiting to
be plucked off and carried away.

"Shit a brick."

FOURTEEN

I grabbed Plover's arm and yanked him to a halt. Then, thoroughly and totally bewildered, I whispered, "That's Paulie's police cruiser over there next to the barn." Before I could choke out any more, Larry Joe and Roy stumbled into us, setting off a less-than-comical chain reaction that almost put all four of us on the ground. Once I'd recovered my balance, I hissed at them to wait and showed Plover the shadowy form with the telltale bubble on the top. "It's Paulie's; I'm almost sure of it. What in thunderation is going on?"

"He's your deputy," Plover said distractedly, gaping at the cabin in front of us.

It was hardly a picturesque Lincoln Log structure surrounded by tidy vegetable plots, whitewashed outbuildings, and animal enclosures — unless you counted the cabin in the last category. The light from windows and innumerable cracks splashed on rusted skeletons of cans and car parts, piles of the more organic variety, and endless scattered debris. The air was ripe with decay. The aftermath of a nuclear explosion came to mind, when only the terminally deformed and walking dead were still around to pick through garbage. A pig grunted on the doorstep, and a few emaciated chickens pecked feverishly for a grub in the baked-dirt surface of yard. The whole scene was pure Early American squalor.

"Someone lives in that miserable thing?" Plover whistled softly through his teeth.

I presumed that was rhetorical. "I just cannot see any reason for Paulie to be here. It doesn't make a toad's hair of sense. You said you thought he had a woman in the cruiser with him —" I stopped, my mouth open wide enough to trap a swarm of flies.

There was someone not too far from us, someone who was hunkered down behind a bush watching Robin's cabin. I screwed up my face and squinted real hard, but I couldn't make out who it was, except it looked too big to be Paulie. I jabbed the Nameless Wonder in the ribs to get his attention, then pointed out the mysterious watcher in the woods. After cautioning Larry Joe and Roy to be quiet, I took out my gun and eased my way around one side while Plover went the other way.

Once he was positioned, I stepped forward and tapped the figure (whom I had now recognized, being a graduate of the academy and all) smartly on the shoulder. "Psst! What in blazes do you think you're doing, Ho?"

"Arly?" Hobert Middleton gasped, clutching at his chest. "Lord, you liked to give me a heart attack!" His piggy eyes were round and yellowish in the darkness, like small harvest moons coming over the ridge. His voice wasn't near that romantic. "Jesus, woman, don't you know better than to sneak up behind a man like that!"

"Now don't you lay into me, Ho Middleton," I said. "Why don't you tell Sergeant Plover and me what the hell you're doing hiding outside Robin Buchanon's cabin? And don't give me any more of that a-good-offense-is-the-best-defense crap! We've heard the whole story of the Drake kidnapping, and your role in it."

Ho stood up and brushed the dirt off his knees, making sure he got every last bit of it. I could almost hear the wheels spinning in his head, but I did want to hear his explanation. Plover looked interested, too, as did Larry Joe and Roy as they joined us. All we needed was a picnic basket and a babbling brook. All we got was the babble.

"Well," Ho said at last, "I guess you could say I'm here out of civic duty, to make one of those citizen's arrests. I didn't mean to give offense earlier, Arly, and I'm right relieved that you and the other police fellow are here to help me out." His tongue flicked out to lick his lips, and he gave Larry Joe and Roy a cold look that could have stopped coffee halfway to the cup. "What happened was I chanced to see Carl Withers in the act of kidnapping some folks that are mighty dear to us all: Ruby Bee, Estelle, and Paulie Buchanon. I have to tell you I was shocked —"

"Who?" I demanded in a muted screech.

He repeated the list, and the identity of the kidnapper. It took several minutes to grasp what he had said, because it didn't make a whit of sense. He kept on with his incredible story, while I sank back and concentrated on breathing. At some point I realized I was leaning on a warm body, but I wasn't in any condition to do anything but lean and keep the lungs going.

From about an inch away from my ear, Plover said, "Where are they now? Have you seen them through a window or heard any of them?"

"And where's Jim Bob?" I squeaked.

Ho admitted he hadn't seen or heard anybody and that, as far as he knew, Jim Bob was still in

Maggody trying to talk to Senator Fiff about the trouble with a capital *T*. No, he hadn't seen hide nor hair of Robin or Drake, and he didn't have any clues to what was going on inside the nasty-looking cabin. No, he hadn't heard any gunfire or screams, neither. He reckoned he'd been there thirty minutes.

He joined Larry Joe and Roy at a distance for a whispered conference, while Plover and I alternately watched the cabin and made puzzled faces at each other. After a few minutes the moon rose, spreading white light across the yard. I wouldn't have been too surprised if a passel of ghosts had wafted in for a dance amid the scraggly rows of corn next to the house. The whole thing didn't make any sense — not any. Well, maybe a little bit.

I went over to Ho and poked a finger in his chest. "I don't think I'm going to buy that story of yours just yet. According to Larry Joe and Roy, you went into town with Jim Bob this morning to do some business. Were you meeting the same fellow you met last night?"

The tongue started flicking like a lizard's. "I didn't meet nobody last night, Arly. I went by my office to write up a credit form so I could settle up the last shipment of trucks. I didn't have an appointment with anybody. And today I just happened to drive by Jaylee's mobile home because . . . " *Flick, flick.* "Well, because I was thinking how sad it was for such a fine young woman to get murdered the way she did."

"Why, Hobert, what a softie you are under that shitheel exterior," I said admiringly. "When did you hear of the tragedy?"

"When I got to the lot this morning. Everybody was talking about it so much they couldn't be bothered trying to sell cars."

"It must have been a real shock for you, too. I suppose you and Jaylee used to have a little something going when the credit forms were all filed away for the night?"

He drew back, his fingers tugging at the end of his string tie. "I beg your pardon, Arly Hanks. I got the best reputation in the county, and I couldn't risk it by courting a married woman, even if her husband was locked up tight in prison."

"Not anymore," I pointed out, gesturing at the cabin. "Carl must have holed up in the mobile home last night and half of today, until he somehow got hold of Ruby Bee, Estelle, and Paulie. Did you know he was there, Ho? Is that why you drove by?"

"How could I know that?" He gulped. The tongue was doing fifty miles per hour in a thirty-mile zone. "I'm not friendly with Carl

Withers's sort. I may have given him a job in the body shop a couple of years back, but I didn't have him over for Sunday dinner just because of it. When he got arrested, I offered to help with a lawyer, which I'd do for any employee of Ho's New and Used. That don't mean I consider them my personal friends."

"I didn't know you paid Carl's lawyer bill," I said, sucking on the inside of my cheek. You may be wondering why I wasn't preoccupied with schemes to storm the cabin to rescue my mother, et al. It didn't look like anybody was going anywhere anytime soon — that's why. Ho's squirmy narrative, on the other hand, was giving me all kinds of ideas. "That was right nice of you. Carl must have been grateful afterward, even though he pleaded guilty and got four years for his trouble."

Ho puckered up and tried to look modest. "He was, and Jaylee came up to me right after the trial with great big old tears in her eyes to thank me kindly for my generous support. I was right touched."

Plover chose this moment to butt in. "Especially when it was a car off your lot that Carl stole and wrecked. You must have been flat out upset when you found out what he'd done."

"I was hurt to the quick, but I didn't let that interfere with my duty to my little family of employees."

"What were you doing the night that Carl was arrested?" I inquired sweetly.

"Why, I seem to recall I was home that night, maybe with a touch of the stomach virus. When the police called, I was tucked in bed with a thermometer and a hot-water bottle."

"You was playing poker with us," Roy said in a low voice. "In the back of my store. You and me, Larry Joe, Jim Bob, and some old boy from over at Hasty that appreciates the opportunity to lose his spending money to us. You remember him, don't you?"

The squirming intensified. "Damn it, I do recollect a poker game that night," Ho allowed with a modicum of grace, if not with much gratitude. "I was still there when the police called to give me the bad word, wasn't I?"

"Nope. You said Robin's latest batch of hooch was made out of skunk piss and was eating through your gizzard so bad you was going home to bed. Jim Bob offered to drive you, but you were too ornery by that time, having donated some of your own money to the house. I guess I thought you were driving the Caddie that night. Didn't know you lied to the police." He glanced at Plover and me to see if we had figured it out by now.

I had. "It was right nice of Carl to drag

himself out of bed and take the rap for you, Ho. How much did it cost?"

There was a ponderous sort of silence, while everybody thought on that one or passed the time with mental estimates. Ho finally threw in the towel with a drawn-out sigh.

"A thousand up front and two thousand when he got out. I didn't expect him to go AWOL from prison and show up right when we had to worry about that EPA fellow from Dallas and Starley City's smartass plan to dump shit in Boone Creek."

"Did you give Carl the money?" I asked.

"Last night he called right before Jim Bob, demanding that I meet him at the car lot with the money. I went ahead and met him, but I had to tell him there wasn't any way I could get hold of that kind of money on short notice. I told him I'd bring it to the Pot O'Gold this morning."

"If that was shortly after eight o'clock, then Jaylee was still alive and at the Pot O'Gold herself. What did Carl intend to do — knock on the door and pretend to be a Latin American political refugee?"

"He'd done something to his ankle that had made him meaner than a polecat in the spring," Ho said, shuddering as he remembered Carl's more descriptive threats. "He was mad enough to kill her in the door without any how-dee-do or anything."

"And that was at eight?" I repeated, wrinkling my forehead as I tried to place everybody – for the umpteenth time.

"Closer to ten. Once he was gone, I stopped in the men's room for a few minutes to wash my hands, then drove straight on over to the Kwik-Screw to meet everybody. I was getting a little bit worried about the Drake fellow in my trunk – I didn't want him to suffocate or anything."

"Tell it to the judge." I turned around to confer with the ranking officer in the investigation, who'd been suspiciously quiet all this time. Because he wasn't there. I finally found him halfway around the edge of the clearing, staring at a shed held together with spit and prayers. "Why'd you run off?" I whispered crossly. "I got Ho to admit to all kinds of criminal activity."

"You were too busy to hear the ruckus coming from in there," he whispered back. "It may be the hostages, one of whom I seem to recall is your mother. Maybe we ought to let them out?"

I couldn't find any fault in that, so I dropped to my knees (I love a little drama) and crawled over to the door of the shed. Plover was hissing like a teapot the whole time, but I was too

276

intent to worry about Sergeant Slow Leak or his objections. I raised the board across the door, gave a push, and ducked in case someone was a mind to blow off any heads in the immediate future. Held my breath, too, so they couldn't take a bead on me. I learned all that at the academy.

There was a lengthy, hushed conversation in the darkness. At last Paulie came to the door and peered out, his finger cocked to look like he had a gun. "Who's there?" he croaked.

I told him. He shared the news with his inmates, then we all crawled back through the corn until we were out of the light and far enough away for some hugging and kissing. Our ranks had swelled to eight now, close enough for a softball team if anybody had remembered to bring the ball. If you're getting confused, at this point the team included myself, Plover, Larry Joe, Roy, Ho, Ruby Bee, Estelle, and Paulie. It made for a nice reunion.

On one side of me Paulie started explaining to me how he'd been bushwhacked. On the other Ruby Bee assured me in a steady hiss that she'd only been trying to help the investigation, that she'd had the key all the time so it wasn't like it was a crime or anything. Ho wanted to know how Carl's ankle was feeling. In the middle of the whispered babbles, Estelle pointed a bony finger at Ho and told him *she had figgered it out and knew.* I told Estelle we all knew by this time, but I appreciated her efforts to carry forward the torch of justice. I was about to ask Ruby Bee what the hell she'd been looking for at Jaylee's mobile home when the ninth player stumbled onto the scene.

"Jim Bob, what are you doing here?" We all gasped like the a cappella choir at the Voice of the Almighty Lord Assembly Hall.

His Honor couldn't seem to think of an answer, so he settled for a mute shake of his head as he goggled at our intrepid band. His eyes rested on Ho briefly, then passed on to Larry Joe and Roy with a questioning frown. While Larry Joe did some squirming of his own, Roy told Jim Bob that the EPA man was still lost, but Carl Withers wasn't, that he was in Robin's cabin doing God-knows-what with her.

I tapped Jim Bob on the arm. "Kidnapping's a felony, Mr. Mayor." It didn't gall me at all to use his title at the end of that sentence.

Jim Bob breathed some more, his face real pale in the moonlight and looking like it was made out of concrete. I guessed he wasn't prepared to play ball yet, so I joined Plover a few feet away from the others and whispered, "What are you going to do about Carl? You want me to go back to the jeep and radio the sheriff?"

"I think you, your deputy, and I should be able to handle one man," he said. "Do you trust any of those clowns to go back to the radio and let the sheriff know what the situation is?"

That was a tough question. While I pondered it, I heard a soft buzzing noise from the road behind us. It grew louder, until I caught the melody of a hymn and realized someone was humming. I shushed everybody and we all squatted down in the weeds, poking each other to be still and pay attention. I think the Girl Scouts play a similar game, although not in the middle of nowhere in the pitch black, cold night air with an armed convict nearby.

"I see a light," came a melodious whisper from the dark. "Do you think it's their coven house?"

"I don't know," said a second voice. Even though it was a whisper, it carried a load of disapproval. "Watch your step now; I don't want to have to carry you back to the car."

"Oh, my God," Jim Bob moaned from somewhere.

I was upright and flexing my knees when Mrs. Jim Bob and Brother Verber came into view. The former moved in quick little steps, as if someone had inserted an iron rod in a most uncomfortable place. The latter was strolling along, pausing after every step or so to mop his forehead with a handkerchief. Nine plus two. Now we could have the national anthem and an opening prayer before the game. Just dandy.

Sighing, everybody else got up with varying degrees of agility (except Jim Bob, who seemed to be worried about a cramp in his leg) and greeted the newcomers. We ran through the explanations for them, although they seemed sort of confused by the time we finished.

"Where is my husband?" Mrs. Jim Bob demanded through a slit in her lips. The words spurted out between pauses.

"He's around here someplace," I said. Once again I pulled Plover aside for a tête-à-tête. I suggested we send Ruby Bee, Estelle, and Roy back to the jeep to use the radio, and all the other civilians a few hundred yards up the road in case of gunfire. He agreed, so I went back to the group and told everybody what to do.

Everybody obediently scattered, although it was too dark to be sure where they were going. I heard Mrs. Jim Bob pushing through the brush, muttering Jim Bob's name like it was synonymous with Starley City's most famous export. Brother Verber stepped back, but stopped and stared at the cabin as if he hoped he could see right through the walls. Ho's groans mingled with the faintest sound of a hummed hymn.

Sergeant Plover and I took out our guns, made sure they were loaded and ready, and nodded at each other. It was pure cop-show stuff, terribly macho and professional.

Paulie moved beside me and dropped his voice to a barely audible whisper. "Carl has my gun."

"Well, I'm not about to loan you mine, Officer Buchanon."

He shot a quick look at Plover. "He isn't exactly going to recommend me for the state police academy, is he? This whole thing is about the most embarrassing moment of my life; I might as well turn in my badge and ask Ho for a job in the body shop."

I told him it was not the time for career counseling. He continued to mutter under his breath while I consulted Plover about the battle plan, considering the fact we had only two armed officers unless Carl chanced to throw out the gun. In the middle of the discussion, the door of the cabin opened. A woman came out into the patch of hard dirt and stared straight at us.

"I be finished with them. You can have them now."

A truckload of high-school boys squealed into the parking lot of the Kwik-Screw. After a round of punches and jibes, they got out of the truck and swaggered inside to find something to eat, since the Dairy Dee-Lishus was closed down for the night and there was nobody at Ruby Bee's.

There was nobody inside the store, either. The pimply group decided that was a stroke of luck such as they'd never had before, this open invitation to make theirselves right at home without anybody ringing up the cash register or squinting disapproval. One enterprising marauder found Jim Bob's stash of beer behind the canned sodas, which did much to enliven the festive mood. Potato chip and pretzel bags were ripped open and plastic containers of onion dip set on the floor. The magazines with the brown wrappers were attacked with adolescent fervor, as were the little packages of condoms in the back of the drawer. Pretty soon the store was decorated with misshapen beige balloons, streamers of Charmin, and pictures of undressed women from the middle of the magazines.

One God-fearing Christian woman in search

of a gallon of low-fat milk pulled up outside. She left seconds later, milkless and scandalized.

"What if Jim Bob catches us?" one of the boys asked. He was told to have a beer and a Twinkie, which he did. Jim Bob's projected outrage was forgotten in a fine eruption of golden lava.

In the storeroom, Kevin looked up from his business. "Did you hear something?"

Dahlia gave him a look that was blanker than usual, since she was on the distracted side. "No, Kevin, I didn't hear nothing. You jest keep on doing what you was doing – you're getting right good at it, and I'm proud of you."

"Thank you kindly," he murmured modestly.

FIFTEEN

What we found in Robin Buchanon's cabin is, to this day, almost painful to dwell on. Carl Withers was in fair shape; his leg had been wrapped in rags soaked with kerosene and chicken fat, and his eyes were glazed like wax paper from the effects of Robin's latest vintage. His belly was bloated with what we later learned was chitterlings and turnip greens, none of it cooked under the most sanitary conditions. The state board of health might have been unhappy about the skillet, which looked as if it was cleaned once a year, whether it needed it or not, and the inch of rancid lard, which apparently wasn't ever changed. Carl's face was a real peculiar shade of green, sort of mossy or split pea, depending on which moment you glanced at it. His cheeks went in and out like a bullfrog's throat.

The kidnapped bureaucrat was not a pretty sight. For some reason Robin had found it necessary to tie him to the bed in a spread-eagle arrangement that must have hurt like hell. The Spanish Inquisitioners could have learned a lot from her techniques; Drake was about as docile as anything I'd ever seen and way beyond protests. His birthday suit was in dire shape, crisscrossed with red welts and areas where the blood had seeped up in tiny brown bubbles. His eyes didn't see anything, and he seemed unaware of the spit dribbling out of the corners of his mouth. His prick was bright red and about as lively as a plastic worm.

"I had to wash him," Robin said proudly. "He got hisself in a tangle with a skunk, so we all took him out to the yard and washed him in the tub. It took us a long time and a lot of lye soap to scrub him down. We even used the wire brush to clean him good, though he still stinks and probably will for a long time. Carl just needed doctoring and a good meal in his belly."

I gaped at her, then at the feral, filthy children hovering in the shadowy corners of the cabin. They might have used lye soap on Drake, but I figured they hadn't tried it themselves in a blue moon. I almost asked when the anniversary of their annual baths might be, then decided I didn't want to hear the answer.

Swallowing back an acidy taste in my mouth, I told Officer Buchanon to escort Mr. Withers to the edge of the clearing and wait. Carl didn't argue.

Plover finally got control of his jaw, which was about belly-button level. "Why is he tied up like that? Did he attack you or something?"

Robin gave him the look suburban house-wives use on their children when asked why the sky is blue or what God's first name is. "I always do that," she explained with a patient smile. From their lair the children (six or seven – I wasn't sure because I kept seeing more wherever I looked) nodded savagely.

"Do you think he knows we're here?" I asked, moving forward. The smell almost stopped me, but I squared my jaw and bent down to touch the man's shoulder. "Mr. Drake? Can you hear me?"

I'd have gotten more reaction from Raz's bitch – post Mercedes.

"Do you want I should make him talk?" Robin offered. "It'll only take me a minute or two for one of my bastards to fetch a fresh switch off'n the willow tree."

"No, thank you," I said hastily, "I saw a flicker of response. Maybe if we untie him he'll realize what's happening."

Robin scratched her head as she considered

my timid suggestion. "I guess it'd be all right. He ain't no good to me anymores. He's limper than a sow's ear and not even my runtiest girl can get any life out of him." She gave me a woman-to-woman smile. "These fellows from the city can't service as well as my old coon dog when he's a mind to come after me. I don't know how they make so many babies in those big cities, do you?"

That, too, struck me as rhetorical. Plover had untied Drake by now and helped him stagger to his feet. After a wary look at Robin, the Nameless Wonder grabbed the victim under the arms and dragged him toward the door, muttering a polite farewell but not lingering for any responses. I couldn't think of anything to say myself, so I waved goodbye and followed the two across the yard to the road.

Paulie had Carl handcuffed, although the convict didn't look as though he were capable of any violence. Breathing through my mouth, I took one side of Drake and we slowly made our way up the road. Nobody looked back, not even when Robin hollered a friendly caution to watch out for skunks in the dark. We met Mrs. Jim Bob and Brother Verber, gathered them up, and subsequently met Larry Joe, Roy, Estelle, and Ho where the cars were parked.

With icy sternness, I told everyone to drive

back to town and to stay together the entire way. I was going to suggest we reconvene at the PD, but it occurred to me there wasn't any way to cram all the bodies in there, so I ordered them to drive directly to Ruby Bee's and wait for us. Since Ho's car wasn't going anywhere without the aid of a chain saw and a tow truck, I told him to ride with Mrs. Jim Bob and the reverend, who was mopier than a wet cat, for some reason.

"What the hell?" Ho gasped in the middle of my directives. "One of you latecomers must have had a right good time with a goddamn pogo stick on the top of this quality used car. Chief, I want to report vandalism and destruction of property, and I want to know what you aim to do about it." He stuck his head through the car window, then jerked it back so fast he hit the top of the frame. "And theft! I had a bag of money right there on the seat. Which one of you polecats took it?"

"Where is Jim Bob?" Mrs. Jim Bob demanded, still spitting words as if they were watermelon seeds.

I told Ho to can it, then counted noses while Plover dumped Drake in the backseat of the jeep. We were indeed one player short. Everybody yelled for Jim Bob, but we didn't hear anything but owls and echoes. Mrs. Jim Bob burst into tears and flung herself on Brother Verber's chest to caterwaul, but that didn't get Jim Bob out of hiding either. I finally told Roy to drive Jim Bob's four-wheel back to Maggody. I would never admit I hoped Jim Bob would end up in Robin's bed — or stable or whatever; that would have been mean-spirited at best.

Smiling to myself, I told the wagon train to head 'em up and move on out. I picked up a wadded chunk of paper and put it in my pocket. I hate litter. Then we started the complicated task of turning cars around and creeping up the road.

Plover and I did not speak all the way back to the pavement, both of us kind of lost in our thoughts. Larry Joe shoved Drake off his shoulder every now and then, bitching whenever the wind shifted. At one point I called Paulie on the radio to see if it worked, which it did. Ruby Bee grabbed the microphone and started babbling about Jaylee's mobile home, but I switched her off.

Once we arrived at Ruby Bee's, Plover called the dispatcher while I directed traffic inside and arranged everybody at adjoining booths. Drake got one to himself for aromatic reasons. Ruby Bee offered to make coffee, and Estelle went along to help with the cups and saucers. They had the decency to look downright abashed.

The coffee did a lot to ease the memories of the scene in Robin's cabin. After some encouragement, both Carl and Robert Drake were coerced into a semblance of life and persuaded to drink a little coffee. Carl was way too drunk to know what he was doing, and I thought it would take twelve hours in the drunk tank to salvage him. But I wasn't about to let the sheriff have him until I'd gotten some answers.

Drake humbly poured the scalding coffee down his throat, oblivious to whatever pain he was inflicting on himself. At last he seemed to regain consciousness, although he jumped whenever anyone put down a cup or coughed. Likely to do it for a long time coming, too.

"I – I was kidnapped," he said in a hoarse voice. "These men – and another one – they did it. I – I was locked up – in lots of different places – I can't remember exactly – but I –"

"Let me see if I can help you," I interrupted, smiling at him. "You arrived at Maggody Friday afternoon and stopped at the Kwik-Screw for gas and a bite to eat. By a stroke of extremely bad luck, you stumbled into an impromptu meeting of the town council; they were discussing how they could delay the construction contract from being signed until a certain politician could be contacted. That right?"

Drake groaned as he caught a whiff of himself. "That's what they told me right after somebody stuck a rifle in my stomach. I told them it wouldn't do any good at all, but the assholes wouldn't believe me. I never did get my burrito." He looked at his swollen fingers as if they had been glued on when he wasn't paying attention.

"You were taken to the Flamingo Motel," I continued, "where you were stashed in Number Three – with the proprietor's full knowledge and cooperation. A young woman was encouraged to keep you entertained until the vital call could be made to Senator Fiff, and you didn't raise any objections. I'm afraid, Mr. Drake, that the kidnapping charge is thinner than discount-store paint, but you're welcome to file charges with the state police, the FBI, and the sheriff's department. I'd be delighted to assist you with the paperwork."

Plover must have been feeling left out, because he gave me a dirty look and said, "The kidnapping charges will be evaluated at a later time. We need to discuss the murder that happened last night at the motel. Did Mrs. Withers offer to help you escape, Drake?"

"Mrs. Withers my ass," Carl muttered. "Mrs.

Goddamn Whore, if'n you ask me." We hadn't.

"What murder?" Drake squeaked.

I told him about Jaylee. He tried to tell me she was in Little Rock, and it took all of us (à la a cappella choir) to convince him otherwise. Even Sergeant Sincerity Plover had to do some serious nodding and a brief recitation of the reports from the crime lab. Once Drake grasped the point, Plover again asked if Jaylee had offered to help the man escape.

Shivering, Drake gulped down some more coffee. "That's right, Sergeant. We were both afraid that this animal saw us through the window while we were — uh, resting and talking about Mrs. Withers's plans for the future. Mrs. Withers was certain he would misinterpret the scene and break both our necks, so we agreed that the most prudent course of action was to leave town immediately." He squinted at Carl. "Guess we weren't quick enough."

"I'll bet you was talking," Carl said, his face contorted as he attempted a glower. It came out more like an urgent message from his bladder.

"It may have looked different to you, but —"

"Didn't look like nothing to me 'cause I didn't see nothing. But I got a good imagination." He tried to tap his temple, but his finger sailed past and jabbed his nose. "Lissen here, you mother —"

"Perhaps someone else saw you through the window?" I suggested.

Drake shrugged. "I didn't even see the face. Jaylee was — she was facing the window; I was in the bathroom."

"Any of you gentlemen into Peeping Tom games?" I asked, gazing at Larry Joe, Roy, and Ho (but thinking Larry, Curly, and Moe). "Although Mr. Drake insists he and Jaylee were talking, someone at the window might have mistakenly assumed they were engaged in other pursuits. That might have hurt somebody's feelings."

They shook their heads.

I was hoping for an admission of guilt, but it didn't seem likely so I forged ahead, wishing I knew where I was going. "Jaylee received the letter Monday, which precipitated the plan. Ruby Bee and Estelle threw a party. Drake was all packed and waiting for her when the boys here panicked and decided to move him away from town before I realized what was going on under my nose!" The final sentence heated up along the way, and the glare I turned on Ruby Bee and Estelle was a work of art.

"It was all to save Boone Creek," Ruby Bee began bravely. "You can't think I enjoyed trying to run you off, Ariel."

I stared her into silence, then said, "Meanwhile, Jaylee had a private chat with Jim Bob and later went home to load her car. She was also waiting for Jim Bob to show up with a hefty sum of blackmail money so she could afford the cosmetology school and life in the big city. I wonder if he paid her off or tried to brazen it out?" I turned on Mrs. Jim Bob, who was sniveling in the far booth, a pale pink tissue clutched in her hand.

"I don't know," she whispered. "I have no idea where that woman lived, so how would I know if Jim Bob went there to pay her money?"

"Liar!" Estelle chirped, on her feet with her hands on her hips. "While we were on the sofa I found this tissue under the cushion. It's the same color as yours! That proves you were there."

Mrs. Jim Bob gasped as if Estelle had flapped a snake in her face. "That's not mine. She could have bought a box of pink tissues at the store, just like I did."

"This was the only tissue in the entire mobile home. There wasn't a box anywhere, because we searched. The mobile home was clean and neat; the tissue couldn't have been there long." Estelle advanced with a menacing frown, the tissue held in her fingertips. It would have unnerved me. It almost sent

Mrs. Jim Bob into hysterics.

"All right, all right," she sobbed into her tissue. "I happened to overhear the conversation my husband had with that woman during the party, so after he was gone to meet the other men, I drove over to the slut's mobile home to beg her to keep her mouth shut. I knew Jim Bob wouldn't spend a penny to save his reputation – or keep me from being laughed out of the Voice of the Almighty Lord Assembly."

"Sister Barbara Anne," Brother Verber began, rubbing her hand between his own, "you must know I always have had the deepest –"

"Yeah," she muttered as she yanked her hand free. "Anyway, Jaylee wouldn't listen to reason or decency; she said she had to have the money or she was going to stop at Ruby Bee's and shout the news of her impending blessed event, along with the daddy's name. I gave her the money I'd taken from the store."

"So you stopped at the Kwik-Screw to rifle the till," I said. Dahlia hadn't seen fit to drop that bit of information, but I hadn't asked. "What time did you go to Jaylee's mobile home?"

"About nine forty-five, I guess. Afterward, I went to the tabernacle to pray for forgiveness for the sin of stealing. Brother Verber happened upon me, and we knelt in prayer most of the night. It was most uplifting and comforting." She glared at her companion, who shrank into the plastic and nodded.

That seemed to clear them, although I suspected more than pious prayers had been uplifted. I shook Carl's shoulder. "Wake up so we can talk about your little adventures in Maggody."

He opened one eye and gave me a pouty look. "Don't know what you're talking about, woman."

I turned to Plover, but he was leaning back in his chair like he'd decided to doze through my muddlings. Rip Van Plover, I snorted to myself before turning back. "We don't know when Carl arrived in Maggody, but I'd guess it was Monday evening since that's when he called Hobert Middleton. They had their blackmail conversation around nine o'clock, but Ho had to admit he couldn't make the payoff until the following morning – today. Ho went on to meet the others, and Carl went to the mobile home to wallop Jaylee. Was she there?"

"Naw, she drove off just as I climbed the fence out back," Carl admitted with a hiccup. "All the food was in the garbage, but I dug it out and ate something afore I went to sleep. Being an escaped convict ain't easy, you know.

You got to keep moving all the time, and watch for the dogs and helicopters, and –" He gave us a befuddled smile, punctuated with another hiccup.

"Right," I said as I rubbed my chin. It was beginning to look as if none of the Mafia could have killed Jaylee, since she was alive at the time they met behind the Kwik-Screw. I suddenly realized I had an unsightly bulge on my rump and took out the wadded paper that I'd found in the woods. Smoothing it out, I read it under my breath.

"What's that, Ariel?" Ruby Bee asked, joining me so she could read over my shoulder. The woman has some irritating habits. "Why, doesn't that just tug your heartstrings? Poor old Raz is going to have a funeral for Betty at his place, out behind the barn where he buries his animals. It says afterward he's going to serve dessert so everyone can stay and visit. That is just so sweet."

I looked at Paulie. "Raz is taking this thing awfully seriously, Officer Buchanon. I sort of feel guilty about it; maybe we ought to try to find the Mercedes owner and get him to buy Raz a new bitch."

"Sure, Chief. I'll have motor registration run a list of Mercedes first thing in the morning." He managed a professional tone, but he didn't sound real enthusiastic about it. "Do we know what color the car was?"

I looked at him real hard. "You should have seen it when it went through town around ten o'clock. In fact, you should have stopped the car and given the driver a speeding ticket. Kevin Buchanon told Raz the car went through town at seventy miles an hour – why didn't you ticket it?"

"Maybe I missed it," he said, flinching as I kept boring into him. "Looked away at the crucial moment."

"I went through town right fast about that time," Ho volunteered. "I was damn mad about Carl showing up when I was occupied with this other mess. I must have been going about sixty."

"I drove a mite too fast, too," Larry Joe said. "Joyce tore into me about going to the deer camp, and I was repeating the conversation to myself instead of watching the speedometer."

Roy raised a finger. "I ran the signal light on the way to meet everybody. It took me longer than I expected to find my socks, and I eased through the light because I didn't see any police cars parked anywhere around. Damn Mercedes almost ran me down."

"I did, too," Mrs. Jim Bob said. "I'm usually

298

very careful, but I was halfway through the light before I even saw it, my eyes being fogged with tears and all."

"Goddamn woman all the time crying." That was Carl, of course, but he didn't have a car so we didn't pay him any mind.

I held out my hand to Paulie. "Let me see the ticket pad, Officer Buchanon. If you were indeed parked near the signal light, you should have written a lot of tickets last night at ten. At least five that we've just heard about, to begin with."

He looked at me with a sad smile. "Guess I wasn't paying any attention. I was real upset about not passing the state police academy tests. Maybe I was thinking too hard about the future."

"Whose future – yours or Jaylee's? Maybe you were sitting there thinking about how she was off to Little Rock without you. Maybe you were thinking about what you'd seen through the window of Number Three one afternoon. Why'd you go over there?"

"After I showered, I wanted to tell her I might hear something from the state police academy. Her car was parked in back of Ruby Bee's. I heard some giggles in Number Three. Jaylee saw me in the window and said some right harsh things, so I skedaddled away so she wouldn't know it was me. I couldn't ever admit what I saw; she'd have known and hated me afterward."

"Did you figure out Monday that Jaylee was going to leave town with Drake?"

"I sort of guessed what she aimed to do," he said in a soft, childish voice. "I even went by her mobile home to wish her good luck, but I heard Jim Bob in there making wild threats. I went right up to the window and listened while they talked about the baby. It should have been my baby — but she wouldn't let me touch her. She was all the time telling me she couldn't because she was married to Carl."

"Which was a bit perturbing, after seeing her with Drake and then having to listen to her with Jim Bob," I said sympathetically, hating myself all the while.

"She was screwing everybody but me." He puckered up like he was about to cry, then caught himself and looked away. "She was screwing them, and she was going to leave Maggody with one of them. She pretended to be upset when I got my letter, but I could tell she was kind of relieved. God, I hated her for that."

"So when you saw her drive to the motel, you just turned off the radio and followed her, thinking nobody'd ever guess you had left the signal light stakeout?"

He nodded.

"But it wasn't exactly a spur of the moment thing, was it? You'd stopped at home to pick up the crossbow. You made some fine deductions, Officer Buchanon. You would have made a good officer in the county criminal investigation department if you'd settled for the regular academy." My eyes clouded with tears. "Damn it, Paulie —"

Plover stopped me and quietly recited the Miranda to Paulie while the rest of us listened in stunned silence, except for Carl who developed a severe case of the galloping hiccups. After a rousing one he threw up all over the table (did I mention the chitterlings and turnip greens earlier?). At this point the sheriff arrived, along with a herd of deputies. The state troopers were next, with a bunch of customers who'd been hanging around outside. Show time at Ruby Bee's Bar and Grill, but nobody was in the mood. We all stood around being careful not to look at each other.

SIXTEEN

The show went on most of the night, which was hard since I'd been up since the middle of the previous night. Carl was taken away for a free ride back to Cummins Prison for paperwork; Robert Drake was escorted to the hospital in Starley City, the deputies at a prudent distance. The nurses were going to love him. Paulie was taken away to be booked for homicide. He stopped in front of me to give me a real sad look, then left between two deputies. The conspirators went over their stories about fifty times, as a group and individually in the back room. Ho got to recite his story extra times, since it was the most interesting one. He, too, was eventually escorted out the door by grim-faced deputies.

The team continued to deplete. After a conference with the sheriff and Plover, I released

Larry Joe and Roy but warned them to stay in Maggody until we decided what to do with them. As Roy left, he mentioned rent control, which was probably bribery but sounded okay to me. The sheriff sighed and said they'd keep searching the woods, this time for Mr. Mayor himself, but that it was getting real tedious. I wished them luck.

Mrs. Jim Bob allowed Brother Verber to cling to her elbow as they left for some heavy-duty praying over their sins — omission and commission.

Ruby Bee brought me a grilled cheese sandwich and a glass of milk. It was also bribery, but I was too hungry to point it out to her, and bribery sure wasn't the worst crime I'd encountered in the last few days. She sat down across from me and watched me wolf down the sandwich, her eyes about as leery as a chicken spotting the stewpot.

"You still mad at me?" she asked when I was through eating.

"Why shouldn't I be? You committed crimes, lied to your own flesh and blood, got yourself kidnapped by a crazy escaped convict, and managed to utterly humiliate me in your spare time."

"To save Boone Creek." She flared her nostrils at me so I could see how righteous she was. "I told you earlier that I did it so you could swim in your favorite swimming hole, not because I'm some kind of criminal."

"So your motives were pure." I sighed. "Just promise me that you won't ever get involved in something like this again. If you do, I'm going to put you in the drunk tank so fast you'll be spinning for the next twenty-four hours, rotisserie-style."

"Estelle and I were trying to help."

"Just promise and go make some more coffee, okay?" I said wearily. We both knew her promise wouldn't be worth a plug nickel; she and Estelle watched way too many cop shows. My mother, the boob-tube felon. She promised, I shrugged, and she went so far as to have Estelle cross her heart so I could see how sincere they were.

Plover sat down in the seat Ruby Bee had vacated, his expression as worn out as mine and his whiskers giving his face a blue shadow. "You solved the case, Chief. Congratulations."

"Thanks."

"I'm going to swap cars. You want to ride back to the compound behind the sheriff's department?"

"Can't you find it by yourself?"

"I can find it by myself," he said, sounding embarrassed. "I thought you might want to go with me, that's all. We can stop and have some coffee on the way back."

Ruby Bee's Bar and Grill looked dismal in the early-morning light. The plastic booths and bar stools, the dark jukebox, the scattered sawdust on the floor, the long stretch of bar — all of it looked like death warmed over. No honkytonk, no laughter, no clatter of beer mugs, or girls dancing with their eyes closed. I decided I didn't want to stay there anymore, and I was too tired to sleep.

"Do I get a piece of pie for breakfast?" I said.

The child with the shoulder-length black hair lay on its belly on the muddy bank, staring at the paper boat as it floated down the creek. When it bobbled out of sight, another was folded from the endless supply in the paper bag and positioned in the water for the launch. Pirate ships, each one, setting off to attack one of those big boats with all the sails and kill everybody.

"Sixteen men on a dead man's chest," the child sang under its breath. "Ho, ho, ho and a bottle of hooch."

Kevin opened the storeroom door, squinting as the light hit his eyes. He wasn't sure what time it was, but he reckoned it had to be almost six o'clock. He gaped at the unholy mess in the aisles, then went back to the bed of burlap bags and stroked Dahlia's cheek until she opened her eyes.

"What's the matter?" she murmured, giving him a beatific smile that melted his heart like it was vanilla ice cream in July.

He couldn't bring himself to upset her, not when she looked so warm and contented. "Nothing, my little angel."

She belched softly and rolled over. After a moment of hesitation, he joined her.

"John?" I said incredulously. "That's the most boring name in the entire world. There must be seventy million Johns in the country. Do you realize how much energy I expended trying to come up with something a little more intriguing than that? God, ordinary John? Why wouldn't you admit it before?"

His face turned pink. "Maybe to keep you guessing."

"It was an effective ploy," I admitted, turning a little pink myself. "Is this the sort of thing they teach at the state police academy?"

"Not exactly; I suppose I worked this out myself. You're the first woman chief of police I've worked with, and I may have been — well, a bit peremptory, and I

306

want you to know, ah that —"

I took pity on him and interrupted before he fell over his tongue. "I wasn't too professional at times. If we ever work together on a case in the future, I promise to behave. Scout's honor."

"So you're going to stay in Maggody? I rather picture you on the city streets, rushing from a lecture to a symphony. Neon lights and cocktail parties with the elite . . . " Plover — no, John — gave me that broad, lazy grin I was growing fond of.

"I'm not sure Maggody ever washes out of the bloodstream," I sighed, "which is a depressing thought. I'll stay for the time being." It occurred to me that there might be a little excitement in Maggody after all. If nothing else, I could get elected mayor and give myself a raise.

I looked at the freckles dancing across his cheeks, and the flush coloring his ears. Golden brown eyes. If someone would only brush his hair and tidy him up a little bit, he wouldn't look so unkempt. Pushing aside the rest of my pecan pie, I leaned forward to do my duty.

"Your duck's going to turn out real fine, Arly," he said.

"Thank you kindly, John."

The *Mephitis mephitis* (Mustelidae) had had a

307

good night, having lucked into both a nest of quail eggs and a rotten log teeming with fat, tasty grubs. It scratched a hole in the leaves, contentedly curled up to sleep away the daylight hours. It was, therefore, considerably peeved when the shoe stomped down on its tail.

Without missing a beat, it scurried to its feet, swung around, and lifted its tail.

Jim Bob stumbled back, his hand raised to protect his face. But it was way too late. "Aw, shit," he muttered.

THORNDIKE PRESS HOPES you have enjoyed this Large Print book. All our Large Print titles are designed for the easiest reading, and all our books are made to last. Other Thorndike Press Large Print books are available at your library, through selected bookstores, or directly from the publisher. For more information about current and upcoming titles, please call us, toll free, at 1-800-223-6121, or mail your name and address to:

THORNDIKE PRESS
P. O. BOX 159
THORNDIKE, MAINE 04986

There is no obligation, of course.